HENRY NEILSEN

Spice Trader

Ebook ISBN varies according to platform of purchase.

First edition

ISBN: 978-0-6489426-0-3

This book was professionally typeset on Reedsy. Find out more at reedsy.com

To Mr Read,

Perfection is approachable.

Contents

Chapter 1

I first heard of Spice while I was out at some nightclub or other. I'd have a better memory of exactly where if I hadn't been shitfaced three nights a week for six years. There's a point at which every night becomes a blur of lights and thumping bass tones. The cloying press of bodies sweating out the myriad toxins they'd drunk, snorted, smoked or otherwise imbibed didn't change. The faces of the hookups vanished with the hangovers the next day. I couldn't rightly remember where exactly it was, I just knew I'd had enough of paying too much for watered down drinks and I needed a hit.

One of the guys I was out with gave me 'the look' from across the room, and I knew he had something. I extricated myself from the girl I was dancing with and walked towards him. I'd already dropped a bunch of pills; it probably looked like I was having an epileptic fit in forward motion, but it felt smooth at the time. The place had an outdoor smoking area where you could sneak a joint if you were careful, or chat up whoever you'd been dancing with. I pulled out a cigarette and dangled it loosely from my mouth as I stumbled through the press of bodies, feeling for the zippo in my jeans. The security guard at the back door eyed me as I tried to walk past nonchalantly. I pulled out the lighter and flicked it a few times as I walked toward my friends. They were standing up; the seating had been taken long ago by the chain-smokers. It was that kind of a place. They were standing underneath a worn umbrella that bore the label of some middle-market beer.

Jemima rolled her eyes, and I jerked back as she made an attempt to take the cigarette out of my mouth. "Christ, Pete, when are you gonna give that up? Gives you cancer, yeah?"

"Fuck off," I said. I thought it was a bit hypocritical of her; she was no stranger to party drugs after all. Smoking seemed to genuinely disgust her, though. "You got some stuff or what? I was on with that chick in there so you've got to make it up to me." I pretended to thrust my hips at her.

Jem laughed. "In your dreams. You came of your own free will, any nookie you've missed out on is your own fault." She held up her hands, an indication of innocence, thin fingers outstretched. "As it so happens, Pat's given me a treat. Something new." With that, she reached down her top and plucked out a small baggy full of white powder.

"You know I haven't got enough for fucking coke," I said.

Patrick sat up at this. He'd been watching our conversation with dilated pupils, slumped back against the fence. He was blasted in that particular way you can only get when you really work at it, and Pat made a point of keeping a small pharmacy running through his bloodstream. Drugs, for him, were more professional than recreational.

"'S called 'Spice'," he slurred, staggering over, "and it's fucking great."

"Has he had any?" I asked with a sideways look to Jem, "'cause if it fucks me that much, I'm out."

Jemima glanced at Patrick. "He has, but that's not his problem. He's off his brain on Horse at the moment."

Pat was staring at the space in between us. Jem had the baggy proffered to me still. I snatched it from her and snuck it into my jeans before anyone could see what we were doing.

"What's it like? It's not some shit like Krokodil or anything completely evil, right?" I'd seen enough images of the melting skin of Krokodil users to be wary of any new drug on the market. A high wasn't worth losing your teeth, eyes or skin over. I didn't fancy getting lesions or any of the other nasties you got with Krokodil either.

"It's nothing like that! It's good, trust me." Pat had come back to life after I'd slipped the baggy into my pocket. The sidelong glance I gave Jem transmitted my thoughts to her. *Can I trust this?* I asked her silently.

"It's not just chalk wrapped in noodle dust. It's good. Have a go."

I nodded, downed my beer, slipped my finger into my jeans to make sure the baggy was still there, and turned to the bathroom. I'd like to think I'd have been a little more difficult to convince, but I trusted Jem. Pat was trashed, but he didn't seem likely to fall into a seizure or start clawing at his face any time soon.

You can tell when an establishment caters for drug addicts and miscreants as soon as you go to the bathroom. This place knew exactly what people were there for. I heard a rhythmic thud coming from the fully enclosed cubicle next door, along with muffled moans to match. I locked the door behind me and pulled the baggy and my wallet from my jeans. The graffiti on the walls leered down at me, juxtaposing the once-polished concrete floor, damp with the badly aimed urine of a thousand patrons. The place was filthy. Despite this, people in here had been careful to ensure the stainless-steel sink was dry, wiped down, and devoid of any of the nastiness in the rest of the room.

I did my part, wiping down the side of the basin with a piece of paper towel from the dispenser. Next, a fifty-dollar bill and a credit card from my wallet. I pulled them out, and held them in two fingers with the baggy as I returned the wallet to my jeans. I poured an appropriate-looking amount of the powder onto the flat side of the basin. A distorted reflection stared hungrily back at me. Working with careful precision I cut the pile into a line with the credit card. It had a slightly different feel to it than some of the other drugs I'd tried. It was more crystalline but somehow softer, and almost seemed to glimmer at me in the LED light of the bathroom. *Pearlescent,* I'd have called it if I had been able to think straight.

I stretched, rolling my shoulders back, standing as I rolled the fifty. Once that was done, I hunkered over the sink, pushing one end of the rolled-up note to my nose. I sniffed and moved my head along the line in a movement just short of a jerk.

As I walked back out, the taste still strong in the back of my throat, I felt it hit me.

Chapter 2

"There's no downside, then?"

It was the next morning. I was sprawled on the floor of Pat's apartment, nursing a hair of the dog and blithely oblivious to the garbage that was on TV. The hangover was bad, but it was only as bad as the beers I'd had, and I wasn't feeling any of the nasty comedown effects you get from some of the more exotic types of recreationals. We usually did this; Pat somehow kept himself sober enough during the week to make enough money for a pretty sweet pad, so if none of us got lucky it was back to his place for a debrief. A debrief and a lot of greasy food.

Pat hadn't surfaced yet, so Jem and I had helped ourselves to beers. Well, I'd had a beer. Jem preferred cider, and Pat always kept some in the house just for her. Jem cracked her drink before collapsing onto the recliner.

"Not that I can see. Spice is barely something people even know about yet. God knows where Patty got it from, but I want to know his sources. It's pretty awesome." She was still a little jazzed, she'd obviously taken something a little stronger last night.

"Yeah, where *did* he get it, come to think of it?" The night before had been a bit of a blur, and Pat had been pretty far gone by the time the Spice was brandished so there was no way he'd been in a state of mind to reveal his sources. Jem wasn't wrong though. It was *the* best drug I'd tried in ages. Probably ever.

After walking out of the toilet, I'd spent the evening in a little Spice-shaped cloud. It hit fast, absorbing through the mucous membranes like cocaine or MDMA, but then it got you on a level and held you there. It was an exquisite ephemeral floating, a beautiful feeling of resonance with everyone and everything in the room around you. It was like the term 'cloud nine' had come to life in my brain. I'd swept the room, chatting gaily with everyone I could see. I'd jammed out with the second-rate cover band like they were Muse doing an encore, and I'd plied money into the bar like it was my student loan. It had been an amazing night which had only ended because the sun came up and the pub had shut.

"I dunno, but you know Pat. He's got connections. It'll probably be one of his shady workmates." Jemima and I were always staggered at how much cocaine Pat and his colleagues went through.

Still, at least this stuff didn't have the issues that other substances I'd tried had; there was no crippling feeling of suicidal depression for the next forty-eight hours, nor was there a horrible feeling of exhaustion coupled with an inability to sleep. Aside from the hangover, I felt clear headed, stable, and pretty well fine.

"Have you tried this stuff before then?" I asked Jem.

"What? No. First time last night. Why?"

A clamour from the hallway interrupted my train of thought, and Pat's lanky form staggered into the room. He'd thrown on a pair of track pants and a shirt that had more holes than fabric in it. His hair was a tangled brown mop, and there was a sunken look around his eyes.

"Fuck me. What a night," he exclaimed. The fridge clinked and a *fizz-pop* followed shortly after. Pat wended his way through our supine bodies, and muttered another "Oh, fuck," as he sank into the sofa.

Twisting my neck to look at him took my eyes past the daylit window, and I winced as I said, "Pat. Where'd you get that Spice shit?"

Pat barely moved, except to take a swig of what would probably be the only thing he ate or drank until sundown.

"Didn't get it. I made it." he said.

* * *

The lab setup would have been impressive if it hadn't been concocted from such shitty materials. An old ice cream container, two empty bottles of rum, something that looked like the old sieves your mum would use when making cupcakes. It was all cobbled together and hooked up with a bunch of fish tank hoses.

Jemima looked diffident. "Not exactly Walter White, are you?"

Pat took a drag on his cigarette and thumped her on the arm. "It's not like I'm trying to become a drug kingpin. Just trying to get high on my own time and share it around."

We were in the laundry on the ground floor of his apartment. The majority of the setup was in the sink, except for what looked like a baking tray sitting on top of a worn-out laundry basket.

"How'd you find out about it? How'd you figure out how to do it? You're a banker, how did you even know that this was possible?" Sure, it looked genius, but I couldn't believe he'd taken the initiative to set it up. Pat wasn't one to do things for himself if he could just pay someone to do it.

Pat grinned, "Notice how you don't feel like absolute shit this morning, Pete?" He stared as I nodded. "No cloudy head? No 'Oh fuck, my life is a piece of shit, I just want to crawl in a hole and die?'"

"Yeah…"

"That's why Spice is great. No ill effects. *None.*"

I paused. There was no way in hell that could be right. I peered at the cluster of empty containers and vessels in the laundry. It looked just like every school drug program told you a drug den would look like. Hell, when Pat made the first batch I wouldn't have been surprised if it tasted vaguely of rum. He wasn't known for being careful with his recycling.

"I'm not buying it, man. There's no way you can get as high as it made me and it's not gonna mess me up somehow. Besides, how did you even find out about it?"

Pat shrugged, "Dark web."

Jemima rounded on him. "And you trusted what they were saying? Some guy wearing tinfoil on his head and running his internet through an onion router is the one you're believing about whether or not a drug is bad for you? Are you *serious?*"

"Yeah, it's true, there aren't any–"

"Fuck off it's true," Jem interrupted. "Man, I can't believe I let you pump that shit into me last night. Jesus, this is like a bathroom meth lab."

"Hey," I growled, as Pat started to round on Jem, "Get it out of your system. You're fine, don't get arced up about this." I stood between them, pushing gently against each of their chests. This would happen regularly after a night out. They didn't know how to deal with each other when they were strung out.

Jem looked daggers at me, then shoved herself away from me and stormed out of the laundry.

"Fuck this, I'm out. Going home," she called back.

We stood and listened as she thudded around the lounge. A jangle of keys, a soft curse as she tried to find her handbag. I still had my hand on Pat's chest a couple of minutes later, when we heard the front door slam. I felt Pat relax slightly, the edge of tension disappearing from his frame.

I lowered my hand and considered the contraption again. The process looked remarkably simple, once I saw what it was doing. Three bottles looked as though they were distilled and combined into another, and two or three of the containers on the outside seemed to hold extra ingredients that were added afterwards. There were no flames involved, at least not that I could see. There was a towel, and an empty bag of ice, which looked as though it had been wrapped around one of the large ice cream tubs. The tubes went hither and thither, but there was an elegance to the whole set up. I suddenly found it hard to believe that Pat hadn't done his research extensively before he decided to try this new drug. I returned my gaze to where he still stood, regarding me softly.

"This stuff. It's actually not bad for you? Not addictive? Doesn't degrade your brain? Doesn't fuck you up in some other marvellously interesting way?"

He shrugged, "I mean, it's not like it's FDA approved or anything. But nah. All the stuff I've read about it says it basically just... makes you high, and that's it."

Interesting, I thought.

* * *

It was late in the evening when I walked home from Pat's place. It was easy to get home from his house, just a couple of short corners and then a five hundred metre stretch of road. I walked up my driveway as the dusk was casting auburn light onto my dry lawn. The screen door was unlocked, and I pushed and slightly lifted the key in the wooden door to get the thing to unlatch properly.

I stood in the shower for ages, washing the remains of thirty-six hours of bodily abuse off me. Pat's theory that Spice was somehow a wonder drug with no ill effects seemed too good to be true, but I was too worn out to give much thought to it at the time. Eye drops made the bloodshot go away, a bowl of spaghetti and some toast dealt with the growing pangs of hunger. Before long I was on the sofa in my underwear, dreading Monday morning like the rest of society. Angling the remote just right, I switched the TV on.

I flicked through the channels. There was some boring documentary about lizards, a sitcom from the late '90s, a few reality shows, a reporter saying something about metadata retention. Nothing piqued my interest.

Spice was still on my mind. The news yammered in the background, and I turned it down while some moron in a suit talked rubbish about protecting citizens from unsavoury characters. There was *something* there. You couldn't just *invent* a drug with no side effects and treat it like just another pill or powder.

It'd have to be a smarter man than me to figure it out. The noise from the TV continued until late in the night, long after I'd fallen asleep.

Chapter 3

"They're talking about doing *what?*" I asked. It was about half two in the afternoon, and I was bored of standing in the yard at the factory. My head was miraculously clear, with no sign of the 48- or 72-hour-later hangover that sometimes happened. The clarity of mind wasn't exactly a boon to my work; the day got longer somehow, and the inane drivel of my coworkers grated on my nerves more than it otherwise would. Factory workers weren't exactly brain surgeons, but then we didn't have to be. The pile of steel plate we faced at the corner of the yard had to be lugged from there to the table linisher inside, for the machinists to do with what they would. Jake and I would mainly talk bullshit as we hefted the things through the road and into the main shed. Jake was the other labourer on the shift. I'd barely been listening to him; he'd been off on another of his insane conspiracy theory rants, but the last sentence had caught my attention.

"Say that again. They're talking about doing what?"

"Man, it's crazy. Like, we've been subjected to mind-controlling chemicals in the water for years. And you can't get away from it. Every single government has been controll–"

"No, not that. The stuff about the money." I'd heard the conspiratorial stuff every workday for the last three years, and

I was getting over it. He probably ran a dark web router set up similar to the one Pat had found out about Spice on. I wondered vaguely if the two of them had ever conversed online by accident. Probably not.

"Oh," he said, "Well, y'see, the whole world is now this huge net of wires and radio waves, yeah?"

"Sure."

"Well, they want to leverage that. Say you want to buy a secondhand TV from your mate, or whatever. You're going to have to use your phone as a card reader, and it'll automatically send receipts and shit."

I was incredulous. "Uh-huh. Right. And if you pay with cash? And what about receipts and things like that? How is that policed? Besides, what does it even matter? I'm gonna buy a new TV, big deal. Who cares if some random politician knows?"

I always liked ribbing Jake about these things. I swear he'd come to work covered in tinfoil if it weren't for the mandatory protective equipment requirements.

He looked at me like I was stupid. "Man, they're gonna ban cash! You use cash and they'll arrest you! It's gonna be illegal, dude! They'll use your phone to track your every move." He waited as I dropped my plate onto the pile next to the linisher. The machinist gave me a wry grin as Jake deposited his own plate and turned to walk off. *Don't encourage him,* it said, as I followed Jake.

"Whatever, man," I said. Now we were in a conversation, I figured we may as well continue. "Oh, by the way, have you heard of 'Spice'? It's a new... y'know," I moved my hand to my nostril and breathed in sharply.

His hand was in my pocket before I knew what was happening. It fished around and grabbed my phone. He stared at me like I was insane, then threw the phone almost to the other side of the small yard into a stand of long grass. I protested and started towards where it had landed, but he stopped me.

"What *the fuck* do you think you're doing?" The voice of the conspiracy nut was gone, and in its place was a low growl. "Don't talk about shit like that when you've got one of *those things* on you in my presence." I couldn't help but stutter out a nervous laugh.

"I'm deadly serious," he continued, "You think they put cameras and microphones and GPS units into those damn things for your entertainment? They do it so they can see and hear and listen to our conversations and know where we are when we say them!"

I hadn't seen this side of him before. The man was scared, not just paranoid. "Sorry, man. I didn't think."

"You don't, do you? You just go on believing that this stuff isn't real," he spat, turning back to the pile of plates, adding, "What about this Spice, then?"

I was a little shaken, but reminded myself that he was just a harmless conspiracy nut, and said, "Oh, I tried it on the weekend. It doesn't give you any ill effects after that I can see. It's great. I was going to say, I could hook you up if you were into having a go."

"No thanks," he returned. The cadence of his whole voice, and his entire posture, had changed from the moment he'd thrown the phone. He didn't look like a man so much as a trapped animal, tense and ready to spring. "And Pete?"

"Yeah?"

"Never ask me about things like that while you've got a device on you ever again." He gestured to the grass. "You can go pick it up."

I trudged over to the stand of grass and picked up my phone. The screen wasn't broken or anything. I dusted it off and put it back in my pocket. Jake's glare followed me back to the steel pile, and we didn't talk for the rest of the shift.

* * *

"He *threw your phone away?*"

Pat was cackling quietly in the corner of the room as Jem questioned me about the events of the conversation I'd had in the yard that week. It was our usual Friday catch-up, and the better part of a case of beers and ciders had already been added to the buildup on the coffee and side tables. Jem passed a spliff to me, and I took a drag before continuing.

"Yeah, it was fucking scary if I'm honest. Having a conversation about some pie-in-the-sky conspiracy theory bullshit, then I ask him *one* question and his hands are down my pants grabbing at my phone."

"You should report him to HR," Jem giggled.

"Jemima, if we had a HR department, the pile of porno mags in the corner of the lunchroom would be of far greater concern than anything crazy Jake says." I took another puff on the joint and passed it to Pat, who sat up and said, "It doesn't matter if they heard it. Spice isn't illegal."

Jemima turned, "What?"

Pat shrugged, "Not illegal, man. There's only, like, five places online I've found that show you how to make it, and they're all on dark websites with random data exit points and absurd levels of encryption. Honestly, I'm surprised I even found it."

"Oh, so it's legal because it's so new that nobody knows about it?" I asked.

"Well, yeah," Pat said.

"But, like… it's gonna be made illegal soon, right?" Jemima said, "It's not like they're going to allow people like you to just cook it up in your laundry room or whatever?"

I hesitated . "I'm not sure about that to be honest. I mean, yeah it's a drug and it gets people high. But it's not like it has adverse effects afterward or whatever."

"Like that'll matter. Government doesn't care about it unless it can tax you. Could be a recipe for Advil and unless you asked Johnny from the medicine board very nicely you wouldn't be able to produce squat," Jemima said.

"Ha! You sound like Crazy Jake," I said.

"What? You reckon that this new *easy to produce, non-addictive, low-cost substance that does nothing but make people feel good* is going to come up to the government board on their agenda and they're just going to say, 'oh hey, that's fun. We're fine with that just being around, no need to control its use or distribution'?" Jem ticked each point off of her fingers, "Because if you do, I've got a bridge to sell you."

"I don't know what's going to happen in the future, Jem. I've only got two balls, neither of which are crystal. Just seems like this is a no-lose situation. It's a harmless drug that isn't illegal and isn't hurting anyone. How can it be made illegal? And if it is, how are they going to catch people with it anyway? Pat made it in his basement out of four glass bottles and a fuckin' ice tray. We're not exactly some cartel. Pat, where's that joint?"

Pat was zoned out again on his recliner, beer can in one hand, joint in the other. He came to when I shouted at him, and leaned over toward Jem as she reached for the spliff again.

"You alright, Pat?" Jem said, taking the roll. He was usually quiet and almost always fucked up around us, but I hadn't seen him this far gone this early in ages. He turned toward her, pupils dilated and eyes lazily focusing in on us. When he spoke, it sounded as though his mouth was full of putty.

"Wha–? Oh, yeah, 'mfine. Jus' wen' a bit hard with th' stuff early, 'sall. Gimme a min." He lurched heavily and sank back down into the recliner, grunting slightly. With a second attempt he made it to his feet, and swam with his hands as he staggered to right himself. He stood surveying his situation for a moment. He considered where he was going for an inordinately long time before lurching off in the general direction of the hallway. Jem and I watched after him and listened as he thudded off the walls one by one. The sound of a belt unbuckling told us he'd found the bathroom, so that was something at least.

"Leave the door unlocked!" Jem yelled, then to me, "He passes out in there, you're on duty. No way I'm dealing with it while he's in there with his dick out. I've seen you guys naked enough as it is, I already need counseling."

I laughed, a nervous relief allowing itself to move slowly through me. Jem seemed pretty relaxed, and she was my litmus test. If she thought something was really wrong, then I'd worry. Until then, I trusted that the nurse knew more than I did. The toilet flushed from down the hall, and another series of thuds reported back down to us. Another door creaked open, and then a rattling of drawers. He must have been in his bedroom, probably looking for a lighter or something. I reached to the table, knocking over two beer tins on my way to it, and grabbed my cigarettes. Jem winced.

"Do that outside," she said.

"Jesus, Jem. We're smoking pot indoors. What's your

problem?" I said.

"I don't want the smell of weed around the rest of the apartment block, and I don't want the smell of tobacco around *me*. Outside."

I sighed. "Fine," I stood up groggily, "Come with?" The withering nature of her stare let me know I was in with a very long shot of that actually happening. I shrugged, and headed to the sliding glass door, dodging the dead bottles and cans on the floor.

The cigarette sprang from the pack as I flicked the bottom of it, and I took the zippo from my pocket. I flicked it open, gripping it by the worn and near-forgotten inscription. Leaning on the post on the edge of the verandah, I looked out at the street and took the first drag.

The sun was going down, and the marijuana had just hit my brain to that level where I'd mellowed out and I couldn't find myself thinking of much more than the inherent beauty of the world around us. I watched the hues of the clouds percolate slowly across the sky as the sun sank lower. I saw them reflected in the apartment buildings, and I could see occasional human-shaped blocks silhouetting the windows or balconies. Everyone in those balconies, everyone on the street below, everyone in the entire world was living through something as wild and complex and adventurous as I was. I tried, as I sometimes did when I was stoned, to force myself to comprehend the incredible amount of history that even just the living souls in a place would contain. The vast tree of connections, sprawling out into the universe, full of wasted potential and unintended consequences, of choices and actions and movements. It was a beautiful kind of melancholy, and I let myself sit in it, slowly smoking and enjoying the sense of connected disconnection.

The door slid open behind me.

I turned, the secret smile still on my face, and saw Pat on his feet again. His eyes were far more focused and he had a fresh beer in his hand. He must have taken something to kick him up. Who knew what he kept in his bedroom. Jem followed him out, looking a little more relaxed, like I felt. Pat's eyed darted at her, and before she could get a word out to scold me for throwing the cigarette butt over the balcony, he asked, "So. Where we going tonight?"

"What the hell happened to you?" I asked. "You couldn't spell your own name a minute ago, what gives?"

Pat's eyes shone. "Just threw down a pick-me-up is all. We're cool, I'm feeling fine."

Jem looked at me, then shrugged. "Let's go somewhere where I can be outside. I'm sick of being stuck indoors, and it looks like a nice night."

I thought for a moment. We lived in a mid-sized town in the North of Australia. It was the kind of place that sat in an uncomfortable middle ground when it came to community engagement. It wasn't a small village where everyone knew each other, so there was no community spirit, nor was it large enough for the kind of diversity that led to communal niches. The result was a melting pot of vaguely unhappy people who would all congregate in one place. There was a main nightclub strip, with perhaps fifteen bars and pubs around, which all of us had been going to with alarming regularity since we were flashing fake IDs to bored bouncers in high school. We'd felt like total badasses at the time, but I think the nightclubs tended toward a 'don't-ask-don't-tell' policy when it came to age; we were hardly the only ones that got away with sneaking in.

Further along, there was a more upmarket part of town with

better locations, more interesting interior design, and more expensive drinks. These places had bouncers that seemed as though they'd earned their security certificates, and one or two had large outdoor decks with expansive views over the bay. That seemed like the option. It was pay week, after all. We could be a little grandiose for now.

"Sandy's?" I suggested.

Pat leaped forward at that. Jem shrugged.

"Guess that answers that question," she said.

* * *

Four hours later, I could see Jem, jazzed from five or six of the fruitier varieties of cocktail, entertaining a small crowd of people from the bar stool that served as her pulpit at the edge of the deck.

Sandy's was a beach-themed bar complete with cockle shells and potted palms, the closest thing our town had to a Caribbean nightclub. The old timber deck was painted white, while the tables were painted with a washed out baby blue that was supposed to suggest something of the ocean. The whole effect was somewhat spoiled by the colourful pigments of spilled drinks and the trail of crumbs that still weren't cleaned up from the dinner service. It was a clear night, and the deck was accommodating for any number of partygoers. I caught a snippet of Jem's conversation as I strolled past.

"So I've got my top on still, right, but I've had to take my skirt off and I'm *covered* in shit from where I'd fallen in it. I'm next to a train station at four A.M., everything hanging out from the waist down, washing myself in a sprinkler and just *praying* nobody walks past…"

I walked out of earshot, but I heard a cacophony of laughter follow a few seconds later. She was on top of the world; Jem is in her element when she's got an audience. I was trying to find Pat. I couldn't see him on the deck; he usually didn't come out unless he was having a smoke. I headed back towards the folding doors that led back to the dance floor. The room was lit with the soft glow of LEDs underneath seats and uplighting that reflected off the glittering ceiling. The bassline that had only been a notion out where Jem had been telling her story defined my world in here. It enveloped me, surrounded me and drove a dembow rhythm into my very being. The spasmodic dancing of the crowd suddenly became a vision of ecstatic release, the seething mass grinding to the thumping of the sound system. It was as intoxicating as any drug.

I saw Pat leaning into someone's ear, jaw moving with a sound I had no hope of hearing. The young woman he was talking to wasn't exhibiting the body language of a potential hookup; Pat must be negotiating some business. I saw them hug briefly, and their hands flashed together for just long enough that something could be transferred between them, if you had enough experience. She gave him a cursory smile, then walked away. He straightened and saw me as he turned. I moved toward him, putting my hand around his shoulder to bend his ear.

"Sandy's, man! Great choice!" he said. "Been too long!"

"Yeah dude!" I shot back.

"Where's Jem?"

"Outside. She's telling that story about when she fell in dog shit again." I said.

Pat bent over double. I couldn't hear the laughter but I knew it was there. He had been the first person she'd told, several years ago. It was now a staple of her repertoire; after the initial embarrassment she'd now tell anyone who cared to listen. She was good at the story as well; you only had to be around for the opening lines and you'd get sucked in, and laughing with the rest by the time she told the part where she ended up near-naked in front of her manager at quarter to five on a Thursday morning.

Pat's eyes were the combination of bloodshot and dilated you could only really get if you'd been downing drugs like they were candy. His brief grogginess from earlier in the evening was gone, and in its place was the jovial but still-quiet party Pat. He beckoned me to him again, tears in his eyes.

"Trade's going off tonight, man," he said. I gave him a thumbs-up as he bobbed in time with the bass tone seeping into the rhythm of the room. I leaned toward him.

"You know that stuff we had the other night? That Spice stuff?" I asked . "Do you have any more of that on you?" Pat shook his head no, lowering his stance and raising his arms as the song began to drop. We'd shifted away from the main part of the dance floor, and the two of us were in the grey zone between the stand-and-drinkers and the dancers. Pat didn't seem to care, he was so far gone he wouldn't have noticed if we'd space-travelled.

"Nah man, all out. Can't do big batches with my setup, yeah? Used the last of it with you last weekend," At this he gave me a conspiratorial side-eye and said, "Though if you're looking, I've got some stuff here that'll blow your head off."

I shifted away, trying not to look too keen. There was a small part of any drug taker that knows they're only a short step from being a total junkie, and in moments like these, it manifests in a strange way. *When the offer of drugs comes,* the mind tells

21

you, *act as though you could take or leave the next hit.* You know deep down you'd shoot your own sister, then walk over her body to get at it, but if you just act casual for a moment, you can tell yourself you have control. So, I danced. I let myself feel the thrum of the humanity all around me. I smelled the sweat interspersed with the sweet stench of alcohol being spilled on the dance floor, and watched the bizarre ritual unfold around me. The primal need for release, gathering all these people in a thudding room. I needed a different type of release, and though I watched with manufactured carefree abandon, my eyes never wandered from where I knew Pat was. The hunger in *my* eyes wasn't for the sex or the music or the booze or the sheer reckless abandon of it. It was for the promise in my best friend's jacket.

When enough time had passed, I made my way back to him. Slowly, as if to fool myself into not being too eager. The cacophony of the room seemed to deafen itself compared to the blood in my ears as I got back to Pat.

"Alright man, what have you got then?"

Pat smiled at me and turned, patting his pockets as I followed him to the bathroom. I watched the slight stumble in his steps as he walked along. Man, he really was wrecked. He wouldn't be able to think straight until next Wednesday at the rate he was going. The large blue pictogram of a man was illuminated on a nib wall, and we ducked past it into the bathrooms. Sandy's wasn't as savvy about their pharmaceutically enhanced patrons as the dive we'd been in the week before. There was no private cubicle with clean and reflective basins for the discerning junkie. Into the stalls then. If anyone happened to notice the two of us coming out, they might just assume we'd been giving each other a blowjob. I didn't give a shit. I locked the door behind me. There was none of the raw concrete and graffiti here; the lamp above the bowl was projecting softly up and down over dark grey tiles with impeccably clean grouting. Even the stall walls had a tasteful texture to them. Like anyone cared about that kind of thing in a nightclub bathroom.

"What've you got?" I whispered to Pat. He reached inside his left jacket pocket and felt around, then looked puzzled and took his hand out. Swearing, he tried another pocket, which seemed to yield him more luck. He pulled out a baggy and turned to me.

"First bump?" he offered.

"Nah, wouldn't want to deprive you," I said, pulling a fifty-dollar note from my jeans and handing it over to him.

I have to admit, as destroyed as he was, he still knew how to set up. The guy pulled a makeup mirror from nowhere with a level of deftness and finesse that he'd lacked mere moments before. With smooth movements long committed to muscle memory, he lined up, rolled the fifty into a tight straw and sat it in his nostril.

When he stood there, sweating, pupils dilated and with that desperate smile that only addicts have, I had a moment of pure clarity. The image froze in my brain as he looked at me. Later, I'd wonder if it had been some sort of premonition; that my brain knew what was going to happen and made sure that I had a final, pure image of him. I don't know. All I know is that when I remember him, I remember him in that moment; nothing but a sad angel in a toilet stall, silhouetted against an artless backdrop, fifty dollars in his nose and glistening from what came before. The before that caused the next.

He lifted the makeup mirror to his face and I heard the inhale. He tilted his head back, and with a *whoa, fuck* he handed me the mirror and the note. It had come unfurled in his hand as he passed it to me. I'd need to tighten it again, to curl it into shape. I bent to my task just as Pat said "Oh, *fuck*," more urgently, and stumbled.

The blood was already pouring from his nose, and his eyes were nothing but ink black wells. He staggered as he tried to stand again, but fell against the cistern, splitting his head on the tiles. Part of my brain was cold and uncomprehending as I watched on. The other part of me was in control, already shaking violently as I reached for the bolt on the cubicle door. Pat was spasming, jaw clenching and unclenching rapidly. I could hear his teeth grinding and snapping as I got the door open. I pulled his arm, trying to get him to come with me but he was convulsing and completely unresponsive. I hoisted him underneath his elbows instead. Kicking the door with my back foot, I pulled him into the main area of the bathroom and out the door, willing him to be lighter than he was as we entered back into the milieu of Sandy's main bar.

The bouncer spotted me almost instantly, Pat covered in spit and blood, convulsing on the floor as I held him up. He ran over, and as soon as he was close enough I screamed.

"Hurry up and call a fucking ambulance!"

Chapter 4

The hours after Pat's overdose were as blurry and incoherent as the crystal clarity of the moments immediately preceding it. His body was dragged out to the kerb by the bouncer. The ambulance was already there, or else it took an hour to arrive. I couldn't remember. The world turned to red and blue, the unnatural hues dancing off matte, satin and gloss surfaces. The ringing of the siren had an underlying beat that in my mind resembled the rhythms in the nightclub. The paramedics in the back with me asked a lot of *how long had he been drinking* and *had he taken drugs before* and *how long had he been out when we arrived* and a million other questions that rolled meaninglessly past me and out the back window down the road after I answered them. There's a vague recollection of being placed in one of a long line of identically uncomfortable chairs. The lights were no longer soft, or glowing, or shifting shades of red and blue. There were no almost-intentional silhouettes of ecstatic throes of humanity here. The light was as uniform as it was harsh and uninviting, the colour of infinite wakefulness and sterility. There may have been others in the hospital waiting room with me, I honestly can't remember. My mind had switched off. I was void, I was an echo, and I was alone.

I didn't even realise that I didn't know what had happened to Jem until I heard her voice.

"Pete!" She was in the same slinky black outfit I'd last seen her in when she was holding court at the nightclub, but the woman inside was shrunken, lank and pale. Her eyes peered from sunken black sockets that bore the marks of wet mascara and eyeliner wiped away. I stood up, and I watched her come toward me. Quick strides got faster and broke into a run. She collapsed onto me like a wave on the shore, and I felt her sobbing. I found I was crying too. We held the embrace for a long time.

We didn't speak. I gestured vaguely to a seat and Jem lowered herself into it. I sat next to her and for what felt like hours we were enjoined in our silence, the yawning chasm of stillness saying more than words ever could. After a while she rested her head on my shoulder. One or both of us must have dozed off, because suddenly a doctor was in front of us.

There wasn't an expectation. But I still couldn't have comprehended the solid iron fist that went through my chest when the doctor's apology hit my ears.

"We tried as hard as we could, but we were unable to resuscitate him. If we hadn't been administering CPR on him in the ambulance, it's very likely that there wouldn't have been any life signs when we got him here." The doctor was wearing what must have been a well-practiced mask of grief. I hated that woman, in that moment, in her clean coat, telling me how sorry she was. She didn't know Pat and had no idea what it meant to me that he was dead. A part of me knew that watching a person in your charge die would be hard no matter the circumstance, but right then I just wanted to hurt her. Jem was asking questions next to me, and I heard the conversation like it was happening through a wall.

"Do you know what it was?" she asked.

The doctor consulted her notes, and nodded slightly, "Including alcohol, we found six or seven different drugs active in his bloodstream." She almost managed to keep the scorn out of her voice. "Any two of them in the wrong combination could cause an overdose or a negative combinatory effect, but from the symptoms we believe that he had a large amount of cocaine, which was then mixed with ketamine."

Jemima seemed taken aback by that. "Thank you, doctor. Is there anything we need to do for you now?"

The doctor said no, we were free to go. There would be an autopsy later, and they were trying to notify next of kin.

"Oh, he doesn't have any," Jem said. "His parents... yeah. They aren't around anymore."

Before much longer, we managed to get out of the hospital. The dawn was breaking over the trees lining a park at the end of the street, and the two of us were exhausted. There wasn't anything to say in that moment, so we didn't say it.

There hadn't been any discussion, but my place was closer, so that's where we both ended up. I rattled the key to get it at just the right angle, and we staggered through the doorway. We wandered into my bedroom. Silently, both of us stripped down to our underwear. She crawled under the duvet on one side, and I on the other. We faced away from each other.

She might have slept. I know I didn't, until I did.

Chapter 5

Once you realise how much you need to sleep after a traumatising experience, it becomes an instant addiction for the body. Jem and I didn't wake for anything other than a piss and a drink of water until the following morning.

We woke up wrapped around each other. My left arm was numb from where it was stuck under her side, and I had a mouthful of black hair.

I peeled myself off her and crept from the room to make coffee. She'd have it white with one sugar, myself without the sugar. I knew Jem had a shift at some point today, but she wouldn't be going to work. That could be dealt with later. I went and pulled a spare towel from the clean-clothes basket and hung it up in the bathroom for her. I finished making the coffee, double checking that the milk was in date, and took it back into the bedroom, where I set it down next to her on the ground. I pulled some track pants on, then gently shook her awake.

"Hey," I said, "Coffee."

She groaned softly and opened her eyes. How she saw anything out from under that raven-coloured mess I'd never know. There was a mournful air to the way she sat herself up, then reached down to the coffee I'd left for her.

"Thanks," she said. "What time is it?"

"It's about 7:30am," I said, "on Sunday."

"Fuck," she moaned.

"Yeah. I would have left you, but you probably need to call your work to let them know you need some time."

She balked, as the memory of Friday night hit her again, "Yeah," she said, then softer, "Yeah."

Once we'd dealt with work she set herself up in the shower as I lit a cigarette on the balcony.

Pat was dead. The fact seemed less real now in the light of day than it had in the harsh illumination of the emergency room two evenings ago. I kept feeling for the edges of the emotion I knew should be there, but I couldn't find it. It was like a hollow space where the feeling should have been. A void, carefully cauterized at the edges so all that was felt was the raw rubbing and the thick edge of the scab. The feeling of strangeness, of everything and nothing being the same permeated the morning air as the world woke up around me. I was still in my track pants, standing topless on my balcony. A slight whistle through the awning was the only evidence of the breeze blowing past.

Jem stood behind me. The towel I'd lent her was wrapped around her head and she had stolen one of my t-shirts.

"What are we going to do?" she said. The question had an immediate and intimate feeling as much as it had a vast and empty one. It was as much *What are we going to do today?* as it was *What are we going to do without Pat?*

"I don't know," I said, smoke spurting from my lips in concert with the phrase, "I guess we need to be available to answer any questions?"

"I don't think they're going to be asking us any questions. It's not like they're asking what's happened. It's not suspicious," she said. We knew there would be a coroner's report, and probably an inquiry at the nightclub, but beyond that we had no idea.

"What happens to his house?" I asked.

When Jem thought, her lips pursed slightly, and the faintest of creases appeared between her eyebrows. "I think it goes to public sale if there's no heir and it's not in his will. Do you think he had a will?"

"It would surprise me."

We stood in silence after that. I twitched at first when she rested her head on my shoulder, but then moved so I could put my arm around her. The street was more active now, with cars and pedestrians heading to breakfast, or church. Lilting hints of conversation came drifting over us. We were poised at the centre of a world that was blissfully unaware of our tragedy. Nobody knew of the maelstrom we'd just survived. Nobody but the two of us.

It was Jemima who spoke first. "Pete?" She pulled herself off me slightly and looked up.

"Yeah?"

"I want to visit his house."

Chapter 6

We didn't end up going straight there. Jem had taken off with the clothes that she'd borrowed. She planned on getting changed before coming around. For my part, I'd ended up watching the world from the balcony again. Thinking, smoking, and half expecting Pat to slink up the driveway and tell me it was all a big joke.

I got to the house before Jem. Out of something like respect, I stood at the front fence and waited for her before I went in. Jem, Pat and I had met on the same day; it seemed only right that we said goodbye at the same time. The private goodbye, that is. There would be a funeral, and the two of us would have to be there, but that felt less real than this moment. For the longest time it had been the three of us, and the house visit was about us and not anyone else.

I stubbed my cigarette out on the gate as Jem pulled up. It left a smear of ash. I walked to the car as she popped the boot and removed a pair of moving cartons. Handing me a roll of masking tape, she pulled one of the boxes together, and I fumbled around trying to find the end. Once I'd figured it out, she passed me the partially constructed box for me to tape down and started on the second one.

"I'm not sure what they're going to do with all his stuff," she said, "but I'm sure there are certain things he'd want nobody else to have. You know, things that meant something to the three of us." Her hands moved deftly to the opposite side of the second box that I'd just taped and flipped it rightways. I heard her hands sliding across the side of the cardboard, a soft yet sharp sound. She gestured for me to open the gate, and I held it for her as we maneuvered through. The porch, with the broken couch and the hopelessly grubby side table had seemed like home a few short days ago. Now it was a crypt. Jem put her box down and leaned around the corner to the place where Pat kept his secret key and got the door open. The curtains shifted. She stepped softly on the timber floor. I followed her in, and we put the two boxes down in the centre of the room.

"Okay. So we're just going to find the things that we think he'd want us to have, and keep mementos, yeah?" I said.

Jem nodded. "Start with the bedroom?"

My shrug was all the answer she needed. Again she led the way, holding the cardboard box gently in front of her. I followed her down the hallway, passed the stairs that led to the laundry and turned left into the room.

There are stereotypes that you associate with certain types of people. They may not be necessarily fair, or true, or particularly nice, but their presence cannot be denied. They sit just under the surface of every interaction you have with people; unjustified assumptions just ready to leap at you and make you a sexist, or a bigot. A racist. Transphobic.

In that moment, the assumption that would have leapt to anyone's mind was that of a white, well-heeled twenty something man with a functional drug addiction. The room could not have more clearly belonged to such a man if I had fed the instructions into a computer. With a start, I realised it must have been quite a while since I'd seen his room, despite having been at his house once or twice a week for years. Jem and I stepped through the door into a den. A projector was still lit, two girls frozen luridly in flagrante, burning an image onto the wall and shimmering soft reflections into the rest of the room. The evidence of affluence was there; the bedframe was solid timber and the sheets piled haphazardly on top were linen. The interior wall that contained neither bedhead nor pornography was a false wall that led first to a closet and then an ensuite. The curtains were drawn - luckily, considering the screen - and slivers of light were peeking through the gaps, revealing the chaos on the filthy carpet.

Between the empty bottles and cans, which were an expected feature of this house - Jem and I had made more than a perfunctory effort to see to that - were the roaches and papers and leftovers of what seemed like a thousand joints. The thick, sweet smell of it was sunk into the soul of the space. Jem coughed and walked to the window.

"Hold up," I said, crossing to the body of the projector and unplugging it. The porn disappeared from the screen. Jem nodded and flung the windows open.

Dust blew around the room and we could see that there was more than just joints. His bedside tables were *covered* with the waste of cocaine. Baggies, straws, and thin layers of powder abounded.

"Holy shit." Jemima said.

I was reeling. I had long known that Pat's drug problem was the worst of the three of us. It was hard to miss when you spent so much time with him, but it had slipped by me just how bad it was. Jem was walking into the ensuite and let out a gasp as she rounded into the robe. I followed her in.

There was a cabinet, the kind they use to transport musical equipment like amplifiers and things like that. It sat somewhere between knee and hip height, and was slightly wider than a man, all in black with silver clasps and rivets. Into it were fashioned a series of drawers, and they were labelled according to the drugs they held.

"Fuck. Me." I breathed. "He has *everything* here." It was all neatly catalogued, the only part of his private quarters that had any semblance of order.

Jemima wanted out of the room, I could see. I knew how she felt. It was too soon, and too close, to be finding out just how deep Pat's addiction went. I went back into the main bedroom and picked my box up on the way out.

"Ok. Let's split up. I know I've got some stuff that he gave to me on display in the spare room," Jem said. I nodded.

"I'll check the yard. I think there was some stuff of his out there I'd like to keep."

On the way out to the backyard, I went through the laundry. The Spice distiller was still there, set up on the same basket it had been on since I'd seen it just over a week ago. I stopped and looked at the contraption again. It seemed so unlikely that a man who couldn't be motivated enough to stop burning weed charring his carpet could be cognizant enough to build something like this.

Behind the mess of bottles, there was a small piece of paper nestled against the wall. I reached behind and pulled it out. It was a foolscap page, folded into quarters and crumpled, as though it had been stored in a pocket. I unfurled it. It was three pages, two of typed text and one of diagrams, covered in scribbles and Pat's handwriting. Reading through it, I realised that this was the recipe for the stuff that he'd given me at the pub a few weeks ago. He must have copied them from whatever website he'd found and kept them on him.

When he did this I had no idea; between Jem, myself and his drop-ins for pickups it seemed like he was barely ever alone. He must have had a lot more going on in his life than he let on in the dark hours of the morning on a Sunday. I carefully put the paper back where it had been; it seemed disrespectful to read his handwriting. It was almost as though his thoughts should remain private now, and picking the paper up was somehow invasive.

I could hear Jem rummaging around the spare room. Brought back to my senses, I grabbed my box and headed out the back door.

* * *

Four hours later, Jem and I were back in the living room. It was cleaned up, more so than either of us had ever seen it. We'd had to take the empties and distribute them into the recycling bins of half the street. The carpet was as clean as it would ever get; if I'm being honest it still looked disgusting. The black scorch marks and beer stains and flecks of ground in mud were something neither Jem nor I were going to be able to shift. The couches had come up as nice as could be hoped for, and the stains had cleared off the coffee table as well.

In the centre of the room, our two boxes were about three-quarters full each. I had a set of drawing instruments that I'd given him in high school with crude remarks etched into them, a massive Ferrari flag, the saucepans we'd used when we shared a house together. Some smaller things. A cigarette rolling machine. A busted ukulele that we'd promised each other we'd learn but never did. A series of books with the finale still not released. A whole heap of small projects we'd had, growing up, that for one reason or another were abandoned or forgotten. It was a testament to incompleteness. Of voided ambition and excitement for what could be. I didn't know what I'd do with it, but the thought of those long-forgotten goals being handed to others struck me as wrong.

Jem's box was similar. With her there were small gifts, lots of references to their shared loves, and little items that highlighted their identically ironic outlook on life.

"It's strange isn't it," Jem said, "We've known him for so long. He was... he was always here. And now he's not." Her lip was trembling. I was silent, staring blankly into the now alien space that had been our home base for so long, "There's so much of him. There *was* so much of him. *So much.* He was that guy who could make your whole world come to life. And now he's gone. All the conversations. All his knowledge. All the good times. All the arguments, even. I'd take an argument from him right now. I can't handle only half of the memories of our interactions existing anymore. I can't be the caretaker of those." She looked at me and I could see a distorted reflection of the boxes in the moisture at the edge of her eyes. "Two boxes isn't enough for all the person he was." And with that she was crying.

I reached out to her and pulled her into my arms. I may have cried there, too. I didn't really know. For what felt like the longest time the two of us stood there, embracing. Her head nestled into my shoulder, me staring at the two boxes which were the material from of our memories of Pat. She was right. It wasn't enough.

After a long while, she pulled out of my embrace. We stood,

staring at each other for the longest time. Our eyes flickered occasionally downward, but kept returning to look into each other. I could see her grief drowning into her hazel pupils, and I was being drawn inexorably into it. I reached up and pulled a strand of her hair behind her ear. She leaned into it, and I was holding the side of her head.

Gently, I pulled my hand away, sighed, and stood up straight. "We should probably go," I said.

She fully extricated herself from my grasp, and nodded her agreement. I couldn't read her eyes any more as she bent down to pick up the box. I followed suit.

We left the house without talking.

* * *

Pat made the Sunday-evening news. Someone must have filmed it while I was pulling him outside to where the ambulance had come. It was hardly a sympathetic piece. It was like as soon as someone died of an overdose, the fact that you were talking about the life of a living, breathing human became irrelevant. Instead they used it to campaign for tighter drug control, told kids that the man who died had been evil. That he was nothing but a junkie ne'er-do-well. I watched in disgust, then muted the TV.

It made sense though, I reflected. Drugs, in the manner Pat took them, were never bound to be anything but a negative influence on your life in the long run. Still, I wish they'd have at least spoken about the man that I'd known for more than half my life instead of turning him into some cautionary tale.

My mind turned to the small set up he'd had at home. Aside from the crate full of drugs, the Spice rack was probably the only thing in his house that had seemed deliberately organised. It wasn't illegal. He'd told me it wasn't addictive. It had no side effects. It was a perfect drug. It got you high and that was it. There was something there, I thought. The whole damn drug manufacture and distribution culture was a market for humanity's escapist tendencies. That was harmless enough. It only became a problem when the substances did all the things Spice didn't.

I staggered to the fridge and pulled out a bottle of vodka. I didn't even bother to get a glass; they were probably all dirty anyway. I went back into the lounge and sat on the couch again. To nobody but the silently flickering TV, I proffered the bottle in my right hand. A toast.

"Here's to you, Pat." I whispered before taking a swig. I felt the cheapness of the spirit in the oily feeling after the initial burn. I winced slightly, turned to my side table and pushed a stack of papers onto the floor, replacing them with the bottle. I unmuted the news to get the flood of burning effigies of Pat out of my head.

"...Parliament deliberations are continuing in earnest today as the debate on 'right to search' bills regarding private meta-data continues," the reporter was saying. "It is suspected that the lead of the department of defense will push back strongly against the argument put forward by the opposition that it will lead to unlawful breaches of privacy..."

The screen switched to a balding man in a suit. *Fuck, these people lead boring lives,* I thought as I downed another mouthful. I watched the shrewd eyes of the parliamentarian flickering across the camera, back and forward between the reporter and his invisible audience.

"The fact remains that all the national security issues we

have faced recently, all of them, have arisen from a lack of the intelligence that has been available to us. Metadata and other information held on personal devices will be instrumental in apprehending suspects ahead of time. This will not affect the vast majority of people, and in fact will be effective in making our streets and lives safer for you and your families."

Don't have a family, I reflected. The bottle was being rapidly drained, and I'd given up on putting it back on the side table. I nestled it in my arm, the condensation soaking through my hoodie. *Jem's all I've got now. We were a family, of sorts, but fucks like you don't care unless you're a married couple with a white picket fence and two and a half kids.* I found myself angry at him; this man that I'd never met. He was talking about National Security when my best friend had just died.

In a dim corner of my mind I realised it meant that Crazy Jake at work was right, though he was being paranoid as fuck about it as usual. I vaguely listened through a vodka haze to a few stories about new technology for compression of something or other. Something about celebrities being stupid, and something else about being able to pay for stuff on your phone.

I realised I was bored, drunk, and in need of a cigarette. I left the reporters to tell their inconsequential tales about the world and ducked out to my balcony. I'd left my zippo and cigarette case out there. I slid the door almost shut and leaned against the cream render on the wall.

There were only three cigarettes left in the pack; the warning label winked up at me with a glaucoma-filled eye. *This is bad for you,* it said in a stern voice that was as easy to ignore as ever. I'd been ignoring it since I'd been buying them one at a time at the back fence in early high school, why change now? I flicked the zippo and I caught a reflection of the case in the firelight off the pale walls.

It was barely readable anymore, and if you didn't already know what it was; you'd never be able to figure it out. Pat and I had engraved one for each other in tech class in year ten. There was a teacher there who we thought was cool at the time. Where most other teachers were happy to let Pat and I play the truant, kick us out, or ignore us, this guy was different. Rather than demand from us more than we thought we were capable of, he had this catchphrase. 'Perfection is approachable', he used to say. I don't know where he'd gotten it from; some book or movie probably. In the first lesson in that class for the year, the teacher had stood in front of the class, and given us all tips on strategies for completing our personal projects.

"Don't think that you're going to have the time to make the best project anyone ever has in the world. That's not how this works. The best steelworkers, sculptors, carpenters and workers to have ever lived never had anything go one hundred percent the way they wanted it to. You're not going to be marked on your outcome so much as your process. The process is the important thing, and your project will become as good as your process. It'll never be perfect. Nothing ever is. But perfection is *approachable*."

For some reason, and for the first time, that teacher had said something that had resonated with the two lazy dropout hopefuls that Pat and I had been. We'd gone home that night, and on our walk we'd talked about that phrase *ad nauseum* and its connotations.

We'd both actually tried. I'd made a Lazy Susan, and damned if the thing didn't work brilliantly. Pat had made a coffee table. He'd been so proud of it, and it had lived in the lounge room of his home until it burned down in the fire that had killed his parents. When we weren't smoking out the back, or being dragged by the ear into the teachers' offices, we'd been working on our projects. Both of us suddenly found this *drive* to make, to work at things, to trust process. *Perfection is approachable.* It had become our catchphrase. Our *raison d'être* for school. It had earned both of us distinctions in tech. The first and last time I'd ever received one.

To celebrate our woodworking prowess, we'd decided to invest in a pair of decent lighters, not the shitty plastic ones we'd steal at parties. We showed up one lunchtime and carved the phrase into the lighters. In Latin, because *"Latin is fancy as fuck",* as Pat had said. He'd used an internet translator, so it probably said something more like 'Go close and perfect'.

We told each other that we could do anything if we tried. That we could seek that perfection and be happy that we'd never reach it. That we'd try to hold ourselves to the standard of investing in process, like that teacher had taught us.

These things never last. At least they didn't for us. Turns out, using the lighters for spliffs and cigarettes was a lot easier than being inspired day after day by a shit Latin translation. Within a year, both of us were out of school, living the high life of constant partying. Sex, drugs and rock 'n' roll. Or dubstep, as it were.

Time had taken its toll on the lighter. I hadn't lost it, though. 'Perfection is Approachable' it said, and it was reproachful.

Pat had at least done *something* with his life. He'd gotten the business degree, he'd gotten a job at that bank. He was a druggie fuck-up but he'd at least been moving forward. I thought of my own life. I was working a dead-end job in a factory with a conspiracy theorist and nowhere to go but a chiropractor once I got old enough that the heavy lifting affected my back.

I was idly flicking the lighter on and off, staring at the faded inscription. I took another swig of the vodka and winced at the burn. A boldness took me, and the booze egged me on. I knew what I had to do.

Five minutes later, I was out of the apartment and walking down the street, rain hitting the pavement and reflecting like shattered glass.

Chapter 7

A home can become so strange in the dark and still. Hours earlier the place had been softly lit and eerie, but at least outside it was daytime and the world was filled with noise and haste. Now, the steel and wire fence rose from the black of the lawn. The creak which had been barely noticeable when Jem and I had entered earlier now cracked the stillness in the air. A dog started barking a few houses down.

I couldn't see the unkempt lawn as I walked down the path, but I knew it was there, just out of view of the phosphor streetlight. The rain had stopped now and I could see silver crystals of light on the steps as I ascended to his balcony.

I reached around the corner for the key but it wasn't on the hook. It had fallen onto the ledge. I thought it was odd. I was always careful to put it onto the hook in case it fell to the ground. I grabbed it and pushed it into the door, only to find that the door wasn't locked. It wasn't even closed properly. The latch was gently resting against the architrave. The glass that had been used as a doorstop rolled away noisily as I stumbled on it stepping through the threshold.

Someone was here, I thought. Just like the opportunist scumbags of the town to rob the house of a dead man.

"Hello?" I said. The alcohol in my veins rose hotly, allowing me more bravado than usual. After a few seconds of no answer, I kept going.

I walked past the lounges Jem and I had cleaned up earlier that day and made my way into the laundry where the Spice rack had been.

The laundry was ransacked. The bottles and tubes we'd so carefully cleaned away were shattered, and the cupboards were torn open with towels and bedsheets strewn everywhere. The cupboard underneath the laundry sink had been bent from its hinges and groaned when I tried to no avail to close it.

Whoever had done this hadn't been interested in the gently folded pages at the back of the laundry sink, which was what I'd been looking for. I pulled them from the small gap between the melamine counter and the wall, folded them carefully and put them in my pocket. I flicked the light on and looked around a little more. There weren't any more pages there, just the remnants of the bottles.

I switched the light off and headed back toward the front door. About halfway across the living room I stopped and turned around, my shoes squeaking as I pivoted and stood there thinking. *What the hell had they been looking for?* The TV and sound system were still there, as was the cabinet full of limited-edition figurines Pat had collected. The lounge room looked untouched. Whoever had been here seemed to know that what they wanted wasn't in the lounge.

Stepping into the semi-separated kitchen, I realised it hadn't been spared in the same way the lounge had. It, too, bore the marks of a violent and frenetic search. Plates, drawers and cupboard doors had been flung across the room carelessly. Cereal boxes had been poured out. The fridge had been left alone, I saw as I opened it. The beer was untouched. The place creaked and I jumped, but there was nobody there. It was just the house shifting as it cooled in the night.

I called out again, and again got no response. I crept down the hall and turned left into the main bedroom. Within a few minutes, I'd found what they'd been looking for.

* * *

Once I got home, I hesitated to call Jem. The moment in the house the other day had been awkward. Our emotions had been running high, and if we'd not been standing in the house of our recently-dead friend there might have been an incident that one or both of us would have regretted. Historically, neither of us had gone in for that kind of thing; we liked to keep our sexual and emotional regrets external to our friendship.

It had undeniably been there though. I kept getting drawn back into those hazel eyes of hers, and they had been a prominent feature of the interrupted sleep I'd managed to get the night before. I was hoping to keep any such awkwardness to myself; I didn't want to fuck up my relationship with the only friend I had left.

I eventually settled on calling her. If it was going to be a bit awkward I could handle that, and I trusted myself enough to be able to control my base urges for at least a little while as I told her what was going through my mind.

* * *

She had this furtive knock. If I'd not known better from years of experience, I'd have almost thought it was the wind flicking something against the door.

45

I'd been taking notes on the couch. Pat's Spice recipe was clear enough, but the paper was showing signs of wear and he didn't have the best of handwriting even before you started dealing with the inkblots, ash and beer stains. I'd taken some paper and was methodically taking down all of the diagrams, instructions, ingredients and other by-the-bys that had been scribbled in the margins of the paper. The recipe was simple enough, and it was genius in that I wouldn't have to get any large volumes of restricted chemicals, or have to sign my name at a pharmacy or anything. What wasn't available at the grocery store was available at the hardware store, and if I couldn't find it there an office supply store would have it.

I put the notes down carefully, taking a mental image of my place on the page. I grabbed the half-full beer off the table and ambled to the door. Jem waited until the door was fully open before she entered, staying as far away from me as possible. *Great,* I thought, *so it's going to be awkward then.* She helped herself to a cider from the fridge, popped the can open with a little too much force, and flopped herself down on the opposite sofa.

"What's up?" she said.

I hesitated. Telling her about the break-in might just agitate her. We were neither of us in a particularly stable place emotionally. Maybe it wasn't going to help anything if she knew about the ransacking of Pat's house. The stripping of every room but the living room. How I'd found his road case full of drugs, its drawers strewn everywhere, contents nowhere to be found. My eyes met hers. *Hazel,* I thought, then stared at the floor.

"I went over to Pat's," I said.

She didn't seem that phased. "Oh yeah?" she said, scratching the inside of her arm and looking slightly bored.

"Yeah. There was something I found there," I said, then lost my nerve. I couldn't tell her about the break in. "I found the instructions for that new drug he gave us a few weeks ago. The Spice stuff?"

That got her. She stopped scratching, and leaned out of the chair toward me . "Really? Like a recipe?"

"Exactly that. It's three pages, it was behind that kit he made in the laundry."

She whistled softly, "Shit. That was good stuff. Perfect for a night out when you need to do things the next day. You gonna make some?"

Again, I stopped before answering. This idea had seemed great at midnight when I was half-blind on vodka and breaking into Pat's house, but sobriety had a way of dulling the experience of alcohol-induced genius. "Yeah," I said, "but I was thinking of maybe trying to do some good with it."

"How do you mean?" she asked.

"Well. it's got no downside, right? It gets you high but doesn't mentally fuck you the next day. You don't have to worry about addiction, or overdose, or anything else. Not like meth or anything where you'll feel like ants are crawling on your skin or whatever."

Jem got where I was going with it, "Pat said it wasn't even illegal yet."

I grinned, "I mean it will be. No doubt about it. but I just…" I saw the image of Pat, pink foam and spit on his mouth, convulsing on the floor of the night club, "Nobody should have to go through what Pat did. Nobody should have to do it ever again. That's awful."

There was a silence, then she said, "I mean… have you thought that his death didn't make sense? He was careful. He knew what he was doing. It wouldn't be like him to mix poisons like that. Ketamine and Coke are a bad idea. And he was smart, like."

"I've been thinking about that too," I admitted. There had been moments in the last few days when I thought that maybe there had been something deliberate about the overdose. Had Pat been depressed? He had always been on the quiet side, but the quiet was just a channel for his humour. His short responses and silent presence were calming as much as anything else, and it had never struck me as symptomatic of a deeper underlying issue. Then again, I'd been blindsided by the extent of his drug use, so I could be wrong. There was something from that night that I remembered clearly.

"He reached into his left pocket first," I said.

"Sorry?"

I backed up, "I don't think he killed himself. I don't think it was coerced or anything like that. He was dealing on the night. I saw him slip something to someone on the dance floor just before it happened. I couldn't see what it was he gave her, but it was obvious what was going down.

"Later, when we were in the bathroom and we were getting the stuff out, he was talking about the coke. Said it was mad, would blow my head off. As he was talking, he was reaching into his jacket pocket. The left one. There was nothing in there, so he went to a different pocket."

"And?" Jem said.

"Well, I think the Coke was in one pocket, and the Ket was in another, so he could keep it separate. But he was that blind that he just assumed he'd put it in the wrong pocket. Took it out, snorted the wrong stuff. And you know… boom. Overdose."

My fists were clenched as I stared at my curtains.

Jem stepped toward me. Wrapped her arms around me. I broke. Long, wracking sobs poured out of me as the scene in the bathroom played itself out in my mind, the memory seeming to become clearer with time instead of fading. She said nothing, just held me close. There wasn't the awkwardness as we pulled away this time, and she got a box of tissues from the kitchen and proffered them to me.

"I know," she said softly, "I know."

We both sat on the couch, staring at the spot on the floor that you look at when you're not looking at anything, and took in each other's presence, finding comfort once again in that silence. Pat's silence, it felt like.

"So," I said finally, "I don't want anyone to go through what he went through. Drugs can all fuck right off. I want to make and distribute this Spice stuff far and wide. Help people back on their feet. Keep things happening in such a way that we know that we're actually doing a bit of fucking *good* with our lives."

With that, I took out the lighter. I tapped it on the table twice before setting it down. The faded inscription was facing toward Jemima, the ironically terrible translation not even legible. I told her the story of the lighters, of how for that brief moment, we'd been people of whom our parents would be proud.

"I want to do that again. I want to be the man that Pat and I believed we could be when we were in that Tech class. I want to do some good."

Jem smiled. "Yeah. that'd be good."

"Do you want to give me a hand?"

Her hair fell in front of her face as she nodded.

Chapter 8

It was later that week. I was keeping myself occupied at night by poring over my transcriptions of Pat's work and making sure I hadn't made any mistakes. It was a simple but particular process, and it wouldn't take much to stuff it up. Jem, for her part, had told me she was trying to get in touch with as many of her contacts as she could. "We'll need a customer base, after all," she'd said after I'd begrudgingly forwarded contact details of some of the more unsavoury people I knew. Then we'd been contacted by whoever had had the power of attorney and informed that the funeral was to be on the Tuesday. Ten days after Pat's overdose.

I met Jem at the gate of the cemetery. She was standing silently and watching the small crowd of black-clad people ambling through the entrance. She was so thin she just about blended in with the iron fencing in her funeral dress. Her hair was drawn back in a tight bun, and the simple black outfit clung to her frame, a small cardigan wrapping her shoulders.

"Hi," I said as I approached.

She returned the greeting, then, "You look nice."

"Thanks," I said. The suit was one I'd worn to my great uncle's funeral several years ago and never since. It was decent enough, if a few years out of date. An old pair of school shoes got a new coat of polish, and I'd invested in a new tie and shirt. I was finishing my cigarette as I walked up to her, and she screwed up her nose. I rolled my eyes at her, butted the dart out in a nearby ashtray, and offered my arm before walking through the gate.

The funeral was as you'd expect it to be. Every time I'd gone to a funeral, there had been too much of the *he's in a better place now* or *he was such a wonderful person* or *those who knew him loved him dearly*. I would normally be irritated by this string of meaningless platitudes but in this instance it *infuriated me*. How *dare they* talk about Pat like this? 'He's in a better place'? He's in the ground. That's a shit place to be. 'He was a wonderful person'? I loved the man, but he was hardly a philanthropist. And *of course* those of us who were close to him loved him. For fuck's sake, he was my best friend. Jem's best friend. We'd been all we had for each other for so god-damned long that not having him now was still sending shockwaves through my existence. The guy at the pulpit was talking in that queer, sober tone of all funeral directors. The voice that suggests a deep care and regret, but beyond that quiet facade you know that he's probably doing four of these a day and he's really only giving a shit about the invoice.

I stood in my place, quietly fuming as they beatified my wholesome, loving, flawed, addicted, hilarious, genius friend. Jem stood next to me, hazel eyes swimming as she tried to make no noise with her sobs. I stared at the hole in the ground that was to be Pat's final resting place and tried not to picture him slowly rotting. His memories erased like the shattering of a hard drive, the life and energy and joy that he brought to a place permanently gone, fed to the worms and bugs and all manner of subterranean nightmares.

It was as I was desperately trying to turn my mind from images of worms devouring the memories of my friend that I realised someone was looking at me. I hadn't seen her before in my life, but she eyed me with a soft familiarity as the priest continued his eulogy. She stood only about five foot five with blonde hair. An expensive black overcoat and business slacks with a loose fitting blouse suggested someone with a professional job, but the eyes had a caring depth to them that I could detect even from across Pat's grave.

* * *

There was a tree near the gate where I could lean and watch people I didn't know commune after the funeral. There were people I'd heard of, or met once or twice, but they were largely family friends, or people who had helped him out after the death of his parents. I'd said my hello's and goodbye's, passed on my condolences and left to have a cigarette. I was staring through the grounds, the rich green of the grass punctuated by the headstones and burial mounds, when I heard a voice behind me.

"You must be Peter."

It was the woman from before. She stood only as high as my sternum, but her presence extended far beyond her stature. It wasn't commanding; it was more like she simply read everything about you as soon as she saw you. To her, people were just pages from a book to be read. I felt myself strangely disarmed by her.

"Who are you?" I asked, more rudely than I intended.

The woman didn't answer immediately, and seemed to weigh the question in her mind, before saying "I'm Pat's Aunt Kelly. I don't believe we've met, but he spoke about you a lot."

Holding the cigarette in one hand, I reached with the other to shake hers. "I didn't know Pat had an Aunt. I didn't realise he had any close family left."

Her eyes were warm as she smiled, "Yes. I would believe that. We had a somewhat... strange relationship."

Something about her wasn't adding up to me. Pat and I had been friends for a very long time - it didn't seem likely that he would have just forgotten to mention a relative, especially any relative that he'd been in contact with. He'd barely stayed in contact with *me* for a long time after the death of his parents. It was only the fact that we'd both been slipping into a life of easy hedonism that our lives had remained intertwined.

So who was this woman?

She didn't seem to mind my incredulity. I was still silent and thoughtful, and didn't open up much as she spoke to me as I smoked. She stood astride me, and the two of us looked past the cemetery gates to where my friend had been laid to rest. Despite not knowing much about this woman, I found her presence strangely calming. Her voice had a lilting cadence that suggested structure and security. Her questions were sharp, but not barbed, and she seemed genuinely interested in who I was as a person. When I finished my smoke, she turned to me before saying her goodbyes, and she walked across the field, then got into her car and drove off.

I was still staring at the end of the street where she'd turned off when Jem nudged my elbow and I was jolted from my reverie.

"Ready to go?" She asked.

I nodded, and we started walking to the car together. Before I got in, I looked at her over the hood.

"Did you know Pat had an Aunt?"

Chapter 9

"Another pint?"

I nodded glumly. The barkeep had been gracious in keeping the glass more than half full for me all evening - I'd regret it when I went to pay the tab but I didn't care. In lieu of a wake this was how we would send Pat off. Afternoon drinks in the main room of a dingy pub not far from the cemetery. Jem sat next to me with glassy eyes, hunkered over a cider, the yellow bubbling liquid reflected in her hazel pupils.

I drained the last of my glass just as the barman set the next down, and I watched myself from afar as I placed the empty one down too carefully. It was that level of drunk where you're aware of how far gone you are, but you're powerless to stop it. Everything was happening in a kind of slow motion, and I saw myself as though I was a spectator of my own actions. I was barely aware of Jem sitting next to me and talking even though I was engaging in the conversation. The words were a wash, an auditory foam to the cacophony of the bar, and I lent myself to them only as far as I felt I was willing and able.

She was still talking about Aunt Kelly, who I had stopped caring about long ago. I was drinking with the grim determination that I sometimes got. In that moment I couldn't have told you about the decor, the name of the street we were on, the name of the establishment, none of it. My existence was subsumed by the need for the drink. It defined me, surrounded me and bound me to it. The dizziness and disconnectedness which should have made me feel sick instead made me keep going. Through the drink I was pulling myself apart - my physicality was being separated from my thoughts, and that's what I wanted. I grasped at the pint in front of me and drank deeply, then replaced it, askew on the disposable coaster. Jem's head lolled to one side and I reached out and grabbed her knee reassuringly. *We'll be okay,* my body was saying, as my mind did its best to flee.

I don't have much memory of what happened later that night. The two of us kept drinking, and the barman kept supplying. The funeral clothes must have told him what he needed to know, but he mustn't have been watching as we both went far past the point of sensibility. At some point in the night, he decided that we'd be cut off. I did my best to protest.

It's a blur, but my belligerence got the interest of a couple of the other patrons. They could have been bouncers. Their features are a haze in my memory. I don't even know if there were two, or three, or more of them. I was being strong-armed to the door, yelling obscenities and flailing like a lamb being led to the slaughter. Jem had been ejected far more easily than I, and I have a vague recollection of her sitting in the gutter, dress askew, riding up past her thighs. She might have been crying, I don't really know.

The bouncers, or the patrons, whoever they were, let me go as soon as I was outdoors. I fell heavily onto the concrete and scraped my knee. A bravado came over me, thrown heavily into my inebriation by the adrenaline pumping through the fall. I stood, turned and screamed at the men who had ejected me from the venue.

It was at this point that one of them decided he'd had enough. His first punch landed on the bridge of my nose.

Chapter 10

For the second time in three weeks, Jem and I were in a hospital together. She'd slept off the hangover and come to find me in the outpatient ward. I had a split lip, a black eye, and a number of other scrapes and bruises.

The bouncer, or whoever it had been, had knocked me down with the first two blows to the face, and then kicked me a half dozen times. Between the spikes of pain in my ribs and the blood rushing through my ears I'd heard the manager shouting for an ambulance. I'd been curled into the fetal position on the footpath while the world swam around me. I don't remember what happened to Jem, but I'd been pulled into the ambulance by the paramedics on duty. They'd willed me not to lose consciousness all the way to the hospital, and tried to keep me calm, passing me tissues to stem the bleeding from my lip.

Now Jem sat next to me as I lay in an off-white hospital room. She held my hand as we waited for the result of the scans. They thought my rib might have been fractured. Or my jaw, for that matter.

My phone was sitting on the table beside me, along with a glass of water that I think was meant for Jem, and a nurse call button that was meant for me. The rest of the room was as deliberately featureless as possible. It was as though when you got into hospital it was expected that you'd leave your personality at the door.

Jem's hazel eyes looked at me again, creases of worry over-lining the grief that had stood there for nearly two weeks.

"How are you doing now?" she asked.

I tried to move, but gave up due to the pain. "Uuugghh," I groaned, "These drugs aren't strong enough. Do they have any heroin? May as well get hooked on that." I tried to smile, to show her I was joking.

She was quiet for a moment. "I don't think so, Pete."

We sat there in silence for some time. I don't know how long. Time dilates on opioids, and I had an IV pumping me full of them. Jemima seemed content enough on her part. The chair must have been damn uncomfortable, but she didn't move or complain. I felt bad for her, sitting there like that. At one point I tried to intimate that she could go home whenever she liked, but she shook her head *no* and just stayed there, gently holding my hand. I appreciated it.

After a while I murmured, "What happened to us, Jem?"

"What?" she said, pulled out of her daydream.

"What happened to us? We're nothing. We're the cold shell of what we could have been. we had so much potential and now…" I swallowed. It hurt to talk. "Now we're just two people who were too self-involved to notice that our friend was dying."

Her hair fell in front of her face again as she looked down at her hands. "Yeah."

My lip trembled slightly as I asked, "Is it our fault?"

"I don't know. Maybe. Maybe we've grown up to become exactly the losers they think we are."

Tears were welling in my eyes as I said, "I don't want to be that any more."

"We don't have to be, Pete," Jem replied. Then, more firmly, "We don't have to be."

Chapter 11

I 'd ended up with nothing worse than a couple of minor sprains in my intercostals. The black eye and bruised jaw were ugly and colourful, but nothing more.

Jem had seen me home that night, and we'd stayed up talking for ages. I wasn't allowed to sleep for another few hours due to the concussion, so we had to keep my mind occupied. We spoke of small things, of Pat, of times we'd shared at school or at various nights out. She made me laugh too easily, and my chest would convulse painfully every time my diaphragm contracted. Eventually the talk turned more serious. The question of how we'd set up the Spice trade wound up dominating the conversation, along with what had been going on in Pat's life that we hadn't known about before.

"I'm sorry I didn't tell you about the house being robbed." I said to her. Her eyes turned downcast, and suddenly she was very interested her phone. She didn't look away from it as she scrolled too nonchalantly through her various feeds, "I know you're angry about it. We were just in the midst of all this, and I didn't want to have to throw Pat's place being robbed into the mix."

Her eyes remained downcast, and she shifted uncomfortably. If I looked closely enough I could see the pupils dashing left to right as she read something on the screen. She obviously didn't want to talk about it, so I changed the subject.

"So. Who is Kelly? His aunt? How the hell did we not know about her?" I said, gingerly rubbing my jaw. I was aware that we were reiterating the story from the night at the bar, but I didn't have any constructive memories of it.

This got Jem's attention. "I don't know. We've known him so long, but he's never mentioned this woman . What the hell. She just appeared out of nowhere," Jem set the phone on the table and looked at me. "She obviously cares about him otherwise why even come to the funeral? What was she going to achieve?"

This was the conclusion I kept coming to as well, "I don't know."

We sat quietly. The night outside was filled with the screaming of cicadas, but it was the kind of cacophony that became silence. It was everywhere and so it was nowhere. I reached for the table, where I'd put a glass of water and a blister pack of painkillers. I popped one out and threw it back in my mouth, taking a long swallow from the glass.

"How are we going to do this thing with the Spice?"

Jem perked up, "I've been thinking about that. The size of the setup Pat had at his place? That's not enough. That would net him a couple of grams, tops, based on the instructions you've shown me." She listed off the ingredients and their amounts and detailed exactly how much of what ended up in the final mix. "So your yield is pretty low for the amount of stuff. That's not enough to deal. If we want to do this properly, we need to be able to make a couple of hundred grams at a time."

That was a lot, I thought. Certainly enough to get you into trouble for dealing, if you were dealing something that was illegal. We weren't doing that though. We could make what we liked.

"Alright," I said, "We can do that. We can fit it in the spare room here, yeah?"

"Absolutely," she said. "The built-in wardrobe should be enough to store the ingredients. I guess I'm the one who can go get the stuff, seeing as you're hobbling around like an old man with a bad knee." I slapped at her. She dodged easily, leaving me wincing in pain at the sudden movement.

"Ha! Suck it!" she laughed.

I grumbled as I pushed myself back up on the chair, "Alright. The doc says I'll be able to move around freely over the next few days, then I can work on setting up the first batch."

"Yeah, you can do the cooking," she said.

"You know, we might piss some people off," I said.

"How so?"

"Well, think about it. We're doing this deliberately, and at scale, to stop people from being addicted to drugs. I can imagine there are a whole heap of, I dunno, *drug dealers* who might be a wee bit annoyed with that fact." I said, "And typically, drug dealers aren't the type to take things very well when things don't go their way. Not to mention if the police got hold of it, they might want to head us off at the pass and stop us making it before it becomes easy to find in the community."

Jem nodded, "You're right. I think to start with we keep to the crew we know and trust - I'm pretty sure I can get all of Pat's old contacts, he was the one in the know anyway."

She had a point. Of the three of us, Pat had been the main one with any link to the world of drug trading. I didn't actually know the contacts for any dealers, they were just around at the kind of places I hung out.

That had been the previous week. Since then, Jem had gone

and done the shopping. Even though I knew what we were doing was legal, or at least not yet illegal, there was a pang of worry as I watched her unloading the stuff from the car. What if the authorities found out? What would they do with that information? We were doing our best to do it properly. As it turned out, twenty-litre home-brew tanks were a good size for our purposes, so there were a bunch of those. Some nine-litre mop buckets, and a series of filters, sieves, plastic tubing and pipes came into the house over the course of four or five days. I wasn't much use for the lifting, but I connected everything up, double and triple checking my references to the drawings as I put it all together. It was incredible how difficult it was to keep track of the piping and flow between the tanks when you were dealing with a real system rather than a neat collection of graphite lines. The painkillers didn't help me that much either. Despite being effective for pain relief, they clouded my brain and I had to concentrate harder than usual. Being able to do anything for a long time was difficult while I healed. My body fatigued very quickly, and I'd have to go and sit on the couch for a while. Usually I'd fall asleep again shortly after that, and I'd wake up when Jem came around with another load of equipment or ingredients. The progress was slow but continuous, and after six days we were ready to start our first batch.

We decided to keep it small, just in case we didn't do it right. The recipe called for a total cooking time of around a week, but you didn't have to be present for most of it. Just pouring various items in or out. The only particularly labor-intensive task came on day three when part of the concoction required stirring for some hours; otherwise the reaction would form a layer on the bottom and leave the rest of the mix unreacted.

Jem had helped me with that; the act of stirring put an awful lot of stress on my ribs, and I would have probably passed out had I needed to sit at constant attention next to the tub. Afterwards, she'd sworn and said we needed a robot arm to be able to do that part of it. Several hours of stirring was nothing to sneeze at, particularly when the mix had the viscosity of treacle.

After that, she'd disappeared for a couple of days. I didn't really notice at first, not until it was nearly the end of the batch and I hadn't seen her in a while. I tried calling her and she didn't answer. Not that it mattered much; I could handle the rest of it on my own. I continued for another twenty-four hours, hobbling around my house in track pants. After another night of wrapping cooling cloths full of ice around a barrel, decanting it onto a tray to dry out, and running it through a blender, I had a small pile of white dust.

I was officially a drug manufacturer.

Chapter 12

I had to go back to work the following week. I couldn't lift anything or move around with any sort of great speed. The boss decided to put me at one of the machines. It was my job to load in a small piece of metal, ensure the lathe had it in its grips right, press a button, close a panel, press another button, and wait. One minute and forty-six seconds later, I could open the panel, press the button to loosen the lathe grip, remove the freshly created part, and repeat the process.

It was at this station that Crazy Jake came over and started talking to me. His eyes, always shrewd, were gleaming with conspiratorial knowing when he appeared beside me.

"Oh, hi Jake." I said, trying to make myself appear busy and like I didn't want to hear about whatever he wanted to tell me. Unsuccessfully, it would seem.

"You haven't got any *devices* on you, have you?" he whispered.

"You know we're not allowed them when we're in the machine enclosures, Jake."

He looked relieved, "Good, good. Tell me, have you been following the news at all?"

I had to admit to him that I hadn't. I didn't mention that it was because the spare room that I usually kept as a TV room had been rearranged as a drug lab. It didn't seem appropriate.

"You should keep up, Pete. They're taking away our *rights.* It's criminal!" his voice was sharp but low. I could barely hear it over the whirring of the lathe.

I wasn't in the mood for him today. The days dragged on easily enough when I was able to move around normally. Unfortunately, while I could still do most of my work, it hurt my ribs to do too much lifting or lateral movement, so I was stuck on the machines. This made the days seem even longer, and Jake was just too much to deal with. Usually he was nothing but a slight distraction I could laugh at when I was dealing with a comedown or a hangover, but I didn't want to entertain his bullshit this morning.

"What are you talking about, Jake?" I said, with what I assumed was an air of *fuck off* that anyone could have picked up on. Apparently it wasn't specific enough for Crazy Jake though, who took it as an opportunity to tell me.

"They passed it. They passed the law. The one I was telling you about?"

"What law? When did you tell me? What are you on about?" I said. I couldn't remember the conversation, if we'd even had it at all.

"You know. The one about the *devices*?" he pressed. "They passed the law the other day. The government is now allowed to monitor all the phone calls and data you send and receive... and even record you when you're not using your phone." he leaned in and whispered the last, and there was a fleck of spit that flew from his lips and landed on my neck, just below my ear. I carefully took out the machined metal, replaced it with a new one, and closed the safety panel. Then I rounded on him, lathed metal in hand, brandishing it at him.

"Look, Jake, I honestly *don't fucking care.* In the last two weeks, my best mate has died, I've found out he had a *whole other life* I never knew about, and then I got my ass kicked while I was trying to have a *few drinks* to send off my friend. Whatever the government is doing with my fucking phone calls, it can keep doing. I don't care. I'm not an interesting person. I don't have anything worth listening to. I'm just a regular-ass dude who is having a really bad few weeks." I was up close to him, almost shouting, and he was backing up slightly. I felt pain in my side but I didn't really care, "What's more, you're not an interesting person either. Stop listening to crackpot fucking conspiracy theories, stop pretending like the fucking gestapo is going to come knocking on your or my door any day, and stop bothering me."

I sat back down and turned my back to him. I heard him step back slightly, then, "I just don't want them hearing me."

I'd had enough. "Look, they're not going to hear you! They're listening to every single phone call in the country, and if what you say is true, they're listening to everything else as well. How the fuck are they going to be able to hear anything through all that rubbish? People talk about shit. There's going to just be a government database out there full of video calls between friends talking about the latest talent show. Nobody's going to get in trouble for this. Alright?"

He looked chagrined, "They have algorithms, you know."

"Oh, *fuck right off*," I spat. "Can they search the database without a warrant?"

"I don't know. But it's not a matter of whether they *do...*"

He kept talking. I didn't listen. I pulled the chaff off the latest lathed piece, and kept working. I knew it was my own frustration at being stuck at the lathe that was making my mood worse, but I didn't care.

* * *

Jem was around again that night. I didn't ask her where she'd been - I didn't know why. It somehow seemed rude to ask. She'd just been a solid fixture in my life since Pat's death, and the lack of her presence had left a gap in me that I didn't really want to think too hard about.

She looked tired, if I was honest with myself. Dark bags under her eyes, and her face was even more drawn than it had been while she'd been keeping me awake after the accident. She was wolfing down a burger and fries like she hadn't eaten in a week, and from the look of her frame, I didn't rule out the possibility.

I had told her, as I had always done with her and Pat, about the latest altercation with Crazy Jake. I hadn't mentioned my outburst, though. I was kind of ashamed of it, if I was honest. I was munching on the terrible salad that had come with the fish and chips from the local takeaway that Jem had got for me before she came over. I wasn't sure of the last time I'd eaten something resembling a vegetable, so I was forcing it down myself in a hope that I wouldn't end up looking as gaunt as I felt.

"Do you know if the police are looking into what happened at Pat's?" she asked me. I pulled myself out of my reverie, and looked at her as I processed the question.

"What? Um… no. I haven't heard. The last I heard was that his stuff was being auctioned off. He didn't have a will, and no living relatives or anything. Well, aside from that aunt of his that was at the funeral. Maybe she got them." I pulled a sad-looking piece of lettuce out of the salad and placed it on the side of the plate, "I don't think they're too concerned with what happened there. It was a break-in at the house of a man who died of a drug overdose. I imagine they think it has something to do with debts or something."

She seemed satisfied enough with that answer and changed the subject. "Oh, did you finish our first batch?" she asked.

"Oh, yeah! It looks great. I'm just trying to figure out whether or not to try it… I'm almost certain that I got it right, but you know."

Jem considered this, then grabbed my hand.

"Let's try it together," she said.

"Really?"

"Yeah," she said, "Absolutely. I imagine that it'll be fine. I double checked everything up until a few days ago and I couldn't spot any problems. I trust you."

My heart skipped a beat at that, but I tried not to let it show. It seemed only fair, if I thought about it. It was both of our plan to make this stuff, and I guess that meant that the risk had to be with both of us.

"Alright," I said, "I'll get the baggy."

Chapter 13

"Bacon and eggs?" Jem said from my kitchen.

"Oh my god, that smells amazing," I said, shambling down from my bedroom into the open plan living area. The blankets and pillows that Jem had used on the couch were strewn everywhere, but the kitchen was a hive of activity. She had gone to the store at some point while I was still asleep. I leaned on the counter next to her and watched for a moment as she flipped the eggs and cooked them on the other side for a few moments, and turned the bacon over.

"So. We didn't die," I started.

"No," she agreed, "And I don't know about you, but I feel fine now. It's out of my system. My mind is completely clear."

"Yeah. How long have you been up?"

"Since about eight."

I looked at the time on the microwave. It was just after noon. By my guess, the effects of the Spice had worn off at about two in the morning, and we'd gone to sleep straight after. It was strange how time dilated while you were high. It seems to speed by and slow to a crawl simultaneously, and everything had seemed like the most interesting and best idea in the world. Jem and I hadn't done much, just sat watching the TV. The drug made even that most mundane of events feel fresh and exciting.

I had wondered if my lethargy was me getting over the effects of the Spice, or whether it was just me being lazy. Apparently it was the latter, as Jem looked fresher than she had when I'd seen her the night before.

"How were you when you woke up?" I asked.

"My neck was stiff. Your couch sucks." she said, "But no. Fine. It seems like once it's worn off you don't get any sort of residual effect. And when we did that second line it didn't seem to push us any further than we already were, either."

"Yeah, that's true," I realised, "How this stuff works, I'll never know."

Jem was dishing eggs onto my plate, along with enough bacon to sink a small barge. She'd managed to make it extra crispy around the edges, the way I liked it. I hadn't realised she'd paid that much attention to how I ate my bacon.

"Do you reckon we've got something then?" I asked.

"Oh yeah. One hundred per cent. People are willing to put all sorts into their body chasing a high like this," She said. "We could run the local drug dealers out of a market if we do this smart."

I considered that. "A bag of Coke costs what? Two hundred? Two fifty? Something like that?"

"Something like that."

"Well, with the volume we're able to produce at one time, we can undercut that cost by at least two thirds. We'd be able to price them out, even before we started talking about the benefits of the product. *Jesus,* Jem. we could actually do something good with this."

I pulled cutlery from the drawer for the two of us, and we went and sat on the couch together to eat. As she sat down, she pulled her sleeves halfway up her forearms, revealing fine tattoos in the shape of teardrop leaves. God, she was thin, I realised at once, and her skin looked almost transparently pale. The bones of her wrists were sticking out, and the veins were visible underneath. If I hadn't seen her eat the better half of a farm in the last few hours, I'd have assumed it was anorexia, but her appetite was fine. She put a huge piece of bacon in her mouth, then looked over at me.

"You gunna ead thad?" she asked through her mouthful, "'Cause I didn't mage id for you do stare ad." She chewed and swallowed, then darted her fork to my plate and stole a particularly crispy piece of bacon.

Not anorexia then, I thought, as I tried to rescue my breakfast before she devoured it.

My spare room became a hive of activity. The rest of the Spice was left in the drawer we'd set aside for the completed product, and Jem and I bought ingredients in bulk and moved them into the cupboard. At one point, I was left to my own devices as Jem went to hunt down several of Pat's old contacts. She said she'd check in on me, and sent me a message every couple of days keeping me updated with her progress. It was usually just a tick or a cross emoji; I knew which people she was after on a given day. We'd discussed it before she left, and I had a list on my phone to help me keep track.

For three days she disappeared off the face of the earth again and I couldn't get in contact with her. Given she was going to find a bunch of users, I was slightly worried for her at that point, but figured she could handle herself.

In the meantime, I was trying to find out more about Kelly. I didn't really know where to start, except to call the funeral director. I wanted to find out what Kelly's relation was to Pat, and whether any of what she was claiming was true. It just didn't seem right that Pat had a relative that he'd never told me about.

"I was at the funeral of Patrick Donaldson a few weeks ago," I said over the phone. I was flicking the lighter absentmindedly as I spoke, wearing down the inscription more. *Flick, close, spin,* it went. *Open, flick, close, spin. Open, flick, close, spin.* Each time, not quite getting the spin right so that the open followed smoothly on from it. *Perfection is approachable,* I thought, placing my leg over a burn mark on my old timber coffee table. I finally got through to the man who had presumably presided over Pat's funeral.

"Father Spencer speaking," he said, the smooth lines of deep care in his voice that I'd heard at the funeral long gone. In their place was a gruffness; an air of impatience that redoubled my opinion of his insincerity on the pulpit of my friend's death.

"Hi Father. You presided over the funeral of my friend a few weeks ago. I was wondering if I could trouble you with a question or two."

"What about?" His reply was blunt. This man was jaded to the core. I could hardly blame him. A lifetime of death would do that to someone.

"After the funeral, I met a woman who was a relative of the deceased. Her name was Kelly and I'd like to get in contact with her. I don't suppose you have her details?"

"Unfortunately, young man, we are not at liberty to divulge personal information about the attendees of services. It would be a breach of privacy."

"Yeah, look, I understand that, but I'm wondering if an excepti-"

"I'm going to interrupt you there. We cannot divulge personal information."

Something about his tone set me off, and I snapped at him. "I'm not going to go watch her fuck someone through her bedroom window, I'm just trying to find out who she is."

That didn't help my cause. Bad language never seemed to fly with members of the clergy. "Listen here. I will not put up with such language, and neither will I put up with your unnecessary scorn. We are bound by legislation to protect those who attend our services, and I see no reason to release Mrs Gordon's details to the likes of you." And with that, he hung up.

I dropped the phone onto the couch, "What an *absolute* fuckhead," I said to no one in particular, then heaved myself off to the spare room. I needed to cycle the distillate into a separate container.

It was a few hours before I realised.

* * *

We'd timed the second cook so that we were able to both be there for the stirring step on a Saturday. I was healing quite nicely and I was able to assist with the stirring, which was good.

Jem had reappeared the night before and slept on the couch again. Once more she seemed drained and tired when she showed up, but her spirits were high. I asked if she was okay and she told me she'd had a rough week at work. I tried to see if she'd gained or lost weight and couldn't really tell. It had been too soon since the last I'd seen of her to be able to notice differences like that.

She woke up before me the next day, and we had breakfast before we set up a chair in the spare room, and swapped places regularly as we drew the large timber pole through the vat, mixing the solution slowly.

"So her name is Kelly Gordon," I said. "I'll look her up online. I'm sure I'll be able to find her pretty easily. It's not a huge town." My arms ached as I drew the stirrer through, and a dull pain was starting in my chest. I only had a few minutes left, but I didn't want to hand it over to Jem yet. There was some stupid, mammalian machismo stepping into my mind and taking it over. The kind of archaic hindbrain thinking that says to the male mind *if I demonstrate my raw strength, she'll be impressed.* The realisation that I was beginning to harbour these feelings for Jem in earnest left me embarrassed; there'd been many years where we'd been content as friends. I also didn't want to find that it wasn't reciprocated and lose her because of it.

I was staring at her as I stirred, and she was looking back. She was smiling, too, with a knowing look that made me blush.

"So what are you going to do about Kelly?" she asked as I stared straight into the vat of not-quite-Spice.

I willed the colour out of my cheeks. "I don't know. I just want to find out what she had to do with Pat's life, if anything. If she's full of shit, well and good, but if she did have a relationship with him then I want to know about it. Can you get this?" I said, letting go and rotating my arm to loosen the muscles up again. Jem moved from the chair to let me past, and I felt her fingers brush mine. I shot her a look, but she was staring into the vat and I couldn't tell if it had been deliberate or not. "I also want to know if she found out who broke into Pat's place the other week, and what she knows about what they took."

"You know what they took?" Jem asked, only half interested.

"Do you remember that huge rack mount case that he had? The one full of all the drugs? They'd turned that inside out. There was nothing left in there. Did a number on the whole thing."

"Oh damn," she said distractedly, still stirring the mixture, "And you reckon Kelly knows who did it?"

"She's as good a guess as any. She knows something about Pat that we don't."

"Doubt she knows about that much though," she said quickly, "I mean, we were there all the time. It's not like she's ever just dropped around."

I stood up, feeling for my lighter and cigarettes. They were both on my phone, sitting on the floor. "Yeah, true enough, I guess. I don't know. I'm going for a smoke." Jem glared at me, and I blew her a kiss. She pretended to smack it out of the air.

"I know. Cigarettes are bad. Save your sanctimony. I'll be on the balcony." She rocked onto one hip, leaning on the stirrer, a pouty look on her face.

Four days later we were once again looking at a pile of Spice. It had doubled in size since the first batch, and it had the same pearlescent glow I'd seen for the first time in that pub bathroom with Pat.

"That's... a lot." I said.

"Don't worry about it," Jem said, "we've got buyers already. Half of Pat's guys were willing to pony up for a sample, and the others I was able to argue down on the proviso they pay us back when they inevitably come back for more."

"Well, look at you," I said. "So we've got 203 full gram bags, how many have we already sold?"

"I'm not exactly sure, but more than a hundred," she said. I was impressed; she'd clearly been holding up her end of the operation. Meanwhile, I'd been mainlining painkillers and chasing up leads on how to find this Kelly Gordon. I grabbed my phone and went to the notes page, pulling up the research

I'd been doing.

"So there are quite a few Kelly Gordon's that I've found across various social media sites. I can't figure out which one she is specifically, because whichever she is, she doesn't have a profile photo. I've ruled out the ones with profile pics, but I've not started actually trying to contact any of them. To be honest, I don't know how to go about that." I said, and it sounded more helpless than I liked myself feeling.

Jemima looked at me, and rubbed my arm. "You'll figure it out," she said. "When you find her, let me know, will you? I want to come with you when you talk to her."

I nodded, then shifted my attention back to the pile of plastic baggies.

"Okay, so we're pretty confident we can shift this?" I asked.

"Yeah, absolutely no problem. I suggest we get started on the next batch straight away. That way there won't have to be a lag time between this batch and the next. We can keep our customers happy."

I found it amazing how quickly we'd slipped into this role of drug dealers. Manufacturers. The guys who not only consumed the stuff but made it and made a profit from it as well. It seemed to suit Jem down to the ground. There was an entrepreneurial air to her that I hadn't seen before.

"Alright then. I'll get more ingredients for it tomorrow, and you can start pushing it out to people. Try to keep in the circle of people you know and trust though; dealers aren't going to be happy with us being on their turf and I really don't want to piss them off. I've heard what they do to people."

With a glint in her eye, she took the bags and slipped them into her backpack. She gave me a quick hug, then snaked her way past the coffee table and couch and left.

I walked to the window and watched her start her car and reverse out of the driveway. The house was suddenly too quiet. I held myself against the window frame and pulled up some music from my phone onto my stereo, then wandered into the spare room.

The place was a mess. The home brew barrels were lined with the remnants of the sticky mixtures they'd once held, and the carpet had the residue of the tiny spills I'd made over the course of the latest cook. There was an acrid scent pervading the room.

I sighed and fetched the cleaning equipment.

Chapter 14

What I hadn't been prepared for was how mundane the life of a drug dealer would be. I mean, I knew that the drug we were making wasn't illegal or even particularly well-known yet, but it still struck me as ridiculous that I could be bored by a life of crime.

Everything remained the same. I went to work. I listened to Crazy Jake tell his stories. Apparently the fact that people collected data on phones was a new and foreign one, or at least *this* way of collecting data was especially heinous. He wouldn't shut up about the way that the government was apparently obsessed with taking away our civil liberties and how our right to not be electronically tracked was the first sign of our inevitable downfall and blah, blah, blah.

I was able to ignore it by now though, particularly as I could think about what had to happen with the next batch when I got home. Which part needed decanting, or distilling, or which ingredients needed adding. I found myself looking at the lighter again and again, and thinking about that semester where we'd made the tech projects. I had the long-forgotten feeling of being in control of my destiny. Of achieving. Of doing something worthwhile.

So while Jake ranted about paper money and rights and data

retention and how it all meant the end of the world, I coasted through, blissfully unaware, and kept considering how I could improve the batch. How we could push this wonder drug to methadone clinics, or doctors or other ways to help people overcome their addictions. I thought this as I puffed on my cigarettes at lunchtime and chewed painkillers in the evening and washed them down with beer.

Jem was gone. She was out hustling for us. She'd only got pre-orders for about half our stock, so she needed to find people and places she trusted to be able to offload the rest of it. I didn't have any idea how long that would take, so I wasn't going to push her into getting back in touch until she wanted to. So I spent the evening in the house, alone. I sat on my balcony a lot, spinning the lighter with an *open, flick, close, spin,* and wondering if Pat had wanted this to be what would become of his little Spice operation, with its rum bottles and Pyrex containers. I wasn't sure if he had.

The chair on the balcony where he'd sat so often was resolutely empty, and I found myself thinking of his quiet chuckle one Friday evening. I imagined myself telling him of Crazy Jake's tall tales, and his reactions as the stories escalated. The man sat there in my mind, tossing my cigarettes to me and pushing me to finish my stories. The memory soured on me as I remembered he was gone, and I went back to flicking the lighter, slowly drawing down another cigarette when I saw Jem's car wending toward me. The headlights swung across the stucco walls, showing off the flaking paint and water stains. Before she got out, I saw her lean into the back seat and grab her backpack; the same one she'd put the Spice in a few days ago. I waved to her as she got out of the car and stood up as she walked through the gate, butting out my cigarette on the corner of the balustrade. She bounded up the steps and flashed a toothy smile, before beckoning me inside without saying a word.

I followed her in. Despite the heat and humidity of the night air, she was still in full length jeans and a long sleeve top. Still smiling, she turned and slammed the bag down on the counter, "Guess what?" she beamed. She slid onto the couch backward, like a kid flipping into a pool.

"You... sold it all?"

"Damn straight," she said. "Sold like hotcakes, it did. It was hard to stop people from just taking it off my hands. I sold a bunch of it in the first few hours, then maybe the remaining two-thirds in a day and a half. It's taken the rest of the week to get the last of it shifted, but that's literally only because I ran out of people to call."

"Nice work," I said, walking to the fridge. "Beer?"

"Cider, if you've got one," she said.

"Ah, you know what I meant," I said, pulling a can of cider and a bottle of beer from the fridge and tossing the former onto her lap. I twisted the top of my drink and took a long swallow. "The new batch is still a couple of days off but it's moving along nicely. It's a pretty Zen experience making it if I'm honest. Beats being in the factory, that's for sure."

"Absolutely," Jem laughed, and I watched as she slung her neck back and took a swig. She smacked her lips and sat back up, clapping her hand on her knee. "So, wanna see the proceeds from our little philanthropic adventure?" she asked.

I nodded, and she reached into her backpack. Out of it she pulled one of the biggest wads of cash I'd ever seen. It looked like she'd used the remains of a scrunchy, and hadn't bothered to straighten out or tidy up the notes at all. It was a gigantic mess of notes, sticking out in exactly the fashion of a messy bun, with small sections of scrunchy showing around the edges. She threw it onto the table, where it landed with a heavy *thwack.*

I must have looked like a cartoon character, standing there mouth agape, shifting my eyes between Jem's face and the wad on the coffee table. The notes were mainly small, tens and twenties, but here and there were the obvious fifty or even a hundred.

"Holy shit. This is how much money we made?"

"That's how much *you* made." she slapped the side of the beat-up old backpack. It was only now that I saw the sides of it bulging. "I already took out all the costs for setup, like the hosing and the first round of ingredients."

I was spinning my lighter frantically in my hand, trying to work out the maths of it, the return we'd made on just one batch of the stuff. I drained the beer, then set it down carefully on the table next to the pile of cash.

"Holy fuck," I said.

I couldn't stop staring at it even as I walked back from the living room to the fridge to get another drink. It probably wasn't as much money as the volume of the wad seemed to suggest; it looked like such a significant portion of the crappy coffee table that it struck me as so much.

"So how much money is there?" I said.

"Your share, after expenses including setup, ingredients, petrol for me to drive around town, all that stuff? Around fifteen grand."

I was right. Fifteen grand wasn't a huge amount of money, all told. The speed at which I'd attained it was what was blowing me away. Working forty hours a week at a factory as a labourer, it would take me just over four months to earn that, and Jem must take even longer as a casual nurse. We'd knocked this out in two weeks, all told, and we'd be able to get a rolling production going and make that much money each week.

I sat down on the arm of the couch, next to where Jem sat beaming at me. I couldn't help but beam right back; I realised I hadn't seen her so happy since Pat's death. The tiredness around her eyes was gone, though she still looked stick-thin and drained. The skin structure of her face had drawn down, probably from working long hours shifting the Spice. She took a sip from the cider and turned slyly to me.

"So, are we celebrating or what?" she said, then reached down and grabbed the bag again. She unzipped the front pocket - the small one that didn't hold all the cash - and fished around inside. Triumphantly, she pulled a baggy of Spice out and waggled it at me. I laughed.

"You kept some?"

"Sure did. Consider it a profit share," she said, heading to the kitchen. She found a plate and brought it back. I watched her affectionately as she poured out a small amount of Spice onto the smooth charcoal surface of my crockery. She reached into the side pocket of her jacket and pulled a credit card from her wallet and went about cutting the spice into lines. Once done, she looked over and pulled a fifty-dollar bill from my stash of money.

"Hey, make sure that you put that back now," I said, "Don't want you ripping me off, you hear?"

She grinned, rolling the fifty, blocking her left nostril with one hand and snorting one of the lines with the note inserted in her right. She sat back, sniffed, then handed the bill to me.

I grabbed it and crouched enthusiastically next to her. The peculiar sparkle of the drug sat proud against the dark grey of the plate, and I drew it into me with a short breath.

Pushing the note back underneath the scrunchy with the rest, I reclined next to her on the couch. I waited patiently, and not for long, before a pleasant wave of euphoria began to overcome me. *And away we go.*

"How are we celebrating?" I said.

Jem stared at me for a while, and I felt a boundless sense of connectivity between us that I didn't entirely attribute to the Spice. My heart pounded, and I felt as though the room was like a containment field for us, and we were two magnets. There were waves tangling just out of view, in a colour we could perceive but not describe. They were a joyous shade of saccharine, and we shrank into blessed obscurity beneath the crackling forcefield that held us, tight and endless. The moment lasted forever, but not long enough, before I heard the voice come through the fog of superfluous joy.

"We should go to Sandy's," it said. Jem said. I'd barely seen her lips move, which was strange as I'd been staring at them for some time.

"Yeah?" a voice that sounded like my own said.

"Yeah. We can show Pat what we've done. What we're doing." she said.

The thought floated through my brain, which was starting to speed up and fire connections all over the place. "It seems right to me. We should go to the place where we last spoke to our friend. We should spend time there, and let him know that we aren't following him down that path yet. We should let him know that we're going to be okay. And that we're doing everything we can to help people." I realised I was staring at the corner of the room, trying to reconcile the angles in the corner with the organic experience of the Spice, and failing with a kind of gleeful frustration.

"Yeah. I want to see him." Jem said. "Well, not *see* him. But you know."

"I know," I said.

"I'll book us a ride."

* * *

Sandy's had a different feel to it from the last time I'd gone there. The euphoria from the Spice was tinged with the slightest melancholy as I remembered the talk on the dancefloor with Pat, after seeing him selling something to some girl I hadn't known. The smile on his face as he'd recognised me, and the way that the three of us had been hanging out as a unit. Nothing would ever be the same.

It did feel right to come back here, though. It had been just over a month since his death, and Jem and I had made huge strides to not only turning our lives around, but improving the life of other addicts through the substance that Pat had shown us. It seemed like a tribute, I thought as I revelled in the pulse of the music and the dance of the light show. I was sucking a metal straw that was stuck into something hypercoloured and sweet, with a toy umbrella and a piece of fruit hanging from the highball glass. I'd had another couple of lines of Spice since I'd arrived, and between that and the booze I had a brilliant buzz going on. As I rocked back and forward I felt I could see the waves of the music dancing through the lasers and lights. I was watching the energy and pent up tension in the thrumming crowd, feeling it flow through me, around me, and binding the room together. *Pat would love this,* I thought. I finished the drink, then joined the throng and was consumed by the rhythm and noise.

Jem came and found me there, what could have been minutes or hours later. She proffered another cocktail contraption with a citrus something floating in it and beckoned me to the balcony. I held her hand as she led me, and I took a long pull on the cocktail as we sat on the same bench she'd been entertaining people at on the night Pat had died. This time, though, we sat on the other side, and for a moment stared wordlessly out over the water. Pat seemed in that moment to be with us, hands in the pockets of one of his old hoodies with the hood drawn up.

"Do you think they named it for Dune?" Jem asked.

"What, Spice?" I said.

"Yeah."

"Maybe. I'm glad we don't need to fight sandworms to get ours. Just gotta stir that big pot all day."

Jem smiled. "Yeah, that's true. I guess Frank Herbert didn't exactly have us in mind when he wrote it."

"'He who controls the Spice controls the universe,'" I quoted. "I don't think we're there yet."

"Hmm," Jemima murmured in general assent, staring back at the water. Next to her, I could have sworn I saw Pat look up from his lap and do the same.

"Jem?" I said. She looked at me.

"Yeah?"

I hesitated, "I think... I don't know. Do you think Pat would approve of this? If he was here now? Do you think he'd be okay with the two of us peddling the thing that we found instructions for at his house after he died?"

She grabbed my hand then. I looked down at it and watched as she squeezed it gently. The effect of the Spice was still present, and I could almost see a cloud of particles flowing in and out of where we were touching each other. A sort of glow, a miniature shockwave where we touched.

"I think we're doing something good. I think we're doing the best we can for the moment, and I feel that if he was here right now, he'd be on board with what we were trying to do." she said. I barely heard it, I was still watching the glowing connection dance in and out and around and between our hands. I looked up and realised she was looking at me again. The hazel in her eyes was dancing and twirling its way toward mine, and the smile was enveloping her entire body, and mine, and seemed to wrap the two of us in an invincible bubble. My breath felt hot in my lungs, and my heart thrummed.

"Do you want to go back inside?" I almost whispered.

"I have a better idea," she said, and the next thing I felt was her lips on mine, her tongue hot in my mouth, and her fingers running through my hair.

Chapter 15

I f we could just get Spice to cure hangovers, too, I thought, after I slammed my medicine cupboard too loudly while trying to get some dissolvable aspirin tablets. The drinks had been as fruity as they had been potent, and my brain was currently trying to fold itself out of my head via my eyeballs. I dropped the two tabs, one into each glass, and filled them with water, carefully maneuvering them underneath the other dirty dishes in the sink so I could get to the tap.

I tried my best not to stomp my way back to the bedroom, and somehow hit every creaky floorboard on the way. I eased the door open and padded over to the bed, propping myself on the corner next to Jem. Her hair was a matted wreck of black, and the little makeup she'd had on was smudged all over her face and on my pillow. She pulled the blankets up over herself and pressed them to her chest with one arm as she reached toward the glass I'd offered her. She was wincing in the sunlight, and I couldn't help but laugh. I'd never seen her like this before and I realised she was an even worse morning person than myself.

"Shuddup," she said, holding the glass as the tablet dissolved, fizzing. She looked at me sheepishly, and I looked back. After a moment we both laughed awkwardly.

"So that was fun," I offered lamely. She twitched with a small giggle, and nodded assent.

"Seemed like a good idea," she agreed.

We sat there in companionable silence for a while. There seemed to be a lot that we could have said, but nothing that needed saying. There was that moment of realisation for both of us, I think, that we'd slept with our best friend, and that some lines could definitely not be uncrossed.

At the same time I felt very comfortable with it. We'd been experiencing much the same trauma after the death of Pat. I wasn't sure whether it would happen again, or whether or not I really wanted it to. The night before had been a whirlwind of Spice and alcohol-fueled exuberance, and it could have simply been the fact that we were finally letting our hair down after a traumatic time.

Or it couldn't. Who knew? I put my hand out on the blanket on top of where her body was hidden underneath. She reached down and gave it a squeeze. I smiled at her, then stood up and grabbed a shirt, my cigarettes, and my lighter.

I turned to the door, heading out to the balcony.

Perfection is approachable. The inscription kept taking on new meaning every few days since Pat's death. Start a new business, but it's a largely untested drug? *Perfection is approachable.* Attend a funeral, but find out you don't know as much about your dead friend as you thought? *Perfection is approachable.* Fuck your best friend? *Perfection is approachable.* I sighed, and took a drag on the cigarette.

I'd need to quit if there was to be any future with Jem. Not that I'd asked her about that just yet, but the more I thought about it the more it made sense. There were no other people in my life, or hers, as far as I knew. She did disappear and show up looking tired after a few days fairly regularly, but I felt as though she'd have told me if she had a guy. I was leaning on the post on the edge of the balcony when she came out, fully dressed, and holding the bulging bag she'd left here the night before. The clothes were rumpled from being on the floor the entire night, and her jacket still smelled slightly of fruity cocktails and stale smoke.

"I've got work later this afternoon," she apologised, "so I'd best be heading off."

"Ah, cool," I said. "Sure thing." The words that had always flown so openly between us were suddenly stilted and strange. "I'll see you later then," I said. "I think I'm going to finish this batch off in a day or two."

"Yeah. Cool. I'll talk to some buyers again," she said, and stepped across to walk down the stairs. I was shifting to watch her go when she turned around and walked back up. She strode toward me and pulled my head down and kissed me hard on the lips. She pulled back after a few seconds and shot me a sultry look.

"Okay," she said, "bye."

I watched her car drive down the street, a smile building all the way from the bottom of my chest to my face until I was beaming out at the street. I finished my cigarette, butting it out on the corner of the balustrade again, as usual. The black mark glowed with small red flecks of ember as I turned to the door that Jemima had left open. I noticed in the doorway a small piece of paper I'd stepped over on my way out. It was folded neatly in half. I bent to pick it up. It was expensive paper, the kind you'd use in an artist's sketchbook or similar, with nice grain and weave to it, and a heady cream colour.

I unfolded it, and my blood ran cold as I saw the nine words that had been printed, all caps, in neat sans-serif font.

WE KNOW WHAT YOU'RE DOING.
DON'T PUSH YOUR LUCK.

Chapter 16

I stood at the base of the stairs to my apartment. My heart was hammering as I squinted into the darkness. I wasn't sure why I was out there. It was as though I expected whoever had written the threat to just wander along the drive and reveal themselves to me and tell me how they had known what we were up to.

My thoughts screamed along, thinking that they must be some acquaintance of Jem's. One of her buyers that wanted in on the action, maybe. There were a few dealers around; maybe one of them had got wind of Jem distributing a new drug and got pissed off at us. I dismissed the idea; none of them knew about me, and there was no way any of them knew where I lived. As far as they knew, Jem was the entirety of the operation; there was no way they'd have known to slip something under *my* door.

I sighed and continued staring down the driveway and out down the street. I was standing in a t-shirt and jeans, and the weather had turned cold. Goosebumps pricked my skin and I flicked my lighter in my right hand. I lit a cigarette, realising on the first draw that my hands were shaking.

My phone was out of my pocket and I was dialling Jem before I realised what I was doing. After all, if I was getting this kind of threat, she probably was as well. I stared at the cigarette in my other hand as I pressed the phone to my ear, willing the glowing ember on the tip to stop vibrating, to stop betraying my own fear. It didn't work.

"Hi, it's Jem here. I might be on shift, or I might just not want to talk. Don't bother leaving a message, I won't check it. Shoot me a text if you want to talk."

I hung up before I heard the tone for the voicemail service and swiped on her contact until I got to the *new message* screen.

Hey, noticed a weird message in the doorway after you left. Wondering if you got something too. Give me a call. I hesitated, wondering if I should make some reference to the fact that we'd slept together not long before. I breathed out unsteadily, then hit send. What was there to say?

A message like that, she'd get back to me as soon as she got it. The streetlight flickered outside my apartment complex, and my heart ticked up a beat. I looked and realised it was only a bird flying in front of it.

I finished my cigarette and flicked the butt away, then climbed the stairs up to my apartment, forcing myself to not look behind me on the way. I closed the apartment door behind me and locked it. I didn't usually lock it.

I headed to bed. I had work tomorrow. Despite that, I lay in bed for hours thinking about the message I'd received.

I didn't think there was anyone outside Jem that had any idea what was going on. The brew kits, the ingredients and everything had all been purchased by her, not me, and none of my neighbours really cared about what went on in one another's apartments - it was the main reason I'd stayed here for so long.

The ceiling had a large dark water mark on it, which I'd

drawn a line on with a sharpie some months ago to ensure that it wasn't spreading anywhere. I stared at the line now, the clear liminality between the light and the dark part of my ceiling. I was trying hard not to make it some naff metaphor for corruption and honesty, but I couldn't help it. The longer I stared, the more a narrative built into my head, which I'd seen run into the ground in various movies and TV shows.

I'd been living this life of corruption and hedonism for years now, and I was mired in the rot of it. Sure, I was trying to get clean but I was really just substituting illegal drugs for one that wasn't yet illegal. And for some reason, there was someone unhappy with the fact that I was doing that. That was the black line, the sharpie. The dark barrier that wanted to stop me getting my life on track.

I couldn't shake the image of Kelly from my head for some reason. It still seemed strange to me that a woman who seemed that caring and thoughtful was in Pat's life. She obviously wasn't part of the lifestyle that had at least partially resulted in Pat's death. She came from somewhere else. The question was, where?

Absent-mindedly, I pulled the lighter out of my pocket again. *Open, flick, close, spin. Open, flick, close, spin.*

If someone knew what we were doing, they must know the reason we were doing it. Was that true? I felt around the thought with my mind, trying to see if there was a logic to it. *Open, flick, close, spin.* There was no reason to believe that, I decided. Even if someone did know about *what* we were doing, there was no way in hell they'd know *why* we were doing it. *Open, flick, close, spin.* They couldn't possibly know that we were doing this to help people. No way to know that we were trying to clean up people the same way that Spice allowed us to clean up ourselves, without having to sacrifice the fun of recreational drugs. *Open, flick, close, spin.* The message hadn't said explicitly that they knew the *why*, just the *what*. Though the *what* seemed enough that a certain type of individual would seek me out. I was competition. *Open, flick, close, spin.* How the hell did they know that I was the cook though? I couldn't imagine Jem talking to anyone about that type of thing with the buyers. It wasn't like this was her first time distributing drugs. *Open, flick, close, spin.* So if they knew about me, they might have known more than I thought they did about the purpose of the enterprise. And if they knew that, maybe they knew the *why*. And if they knew the *why*, they could guess that maybe I was trying to eliminate their business model on a more permanent basis, and as such I'd become a threat.

Open, flick, close, spin.

I checked my phone again. Jem still hadn't answered my text. She had said she had a shift this evening, and the hospital she was a nurse at was strict with their no phones policy. I placed the phone face down on my nightstand, forcing myself to not look at it.

Open, flick, close, spin.

Jem was the face of our business. She was the one who had to deal with the people. She was the one who was out hustling while I was in my pyjamas, eating and stirring the keg full of chemicals.

Open, flick, close, spin.

I stared at the ceiling as comprehension dawned slowly, fog lifting from my mind. If they were going after me, they'd definitely be after the girl who was actually distributing the shit.

Open, flick, close, spin.

If they knew where I was, they knew where she was as well.

Open, flick, close, spin.

She lived in a studio apartment not far from where Pat used to live.

Open, flick, close.

I was dressed and out the door before I had a chance to even put the lighter down.

Chapter 17

I must have broken four or five speeding laws on my way to Jem's place. My piece-of-shit Ford hatch was hardly a powerhouse, but I hadn't spared the horses on the way. I'd been particularly judicious with one red light on the way past the main shopping mall in the North end of town, and I wouldn't be surprised if I got sent a grim-faced, white-knuckled image of myself in short order, along with a fine for running the light.

I pulled up on the side of the road near Jem's apartment block and leapt from my car. Her apartment was on the second floor of a set of brick dwellings that must have been fashionable or cheap about forty years ago. The cracked concrete driveway had weeds growing through it, and the oil stains from the beat-up cars that moved through it reeked to high heaven. I vaulted the balustrade blocking me from the semi-enclosed stairwell and I turned to mount the stairs as fast as I could. The peeled paint scratched my palms as I reeled myself up the stairs, and the steel frame thundered under my feet. I was gasping slightly when I got to her door, and I pulled at the handle as hard as I could.

Nothing. I pounded on the door, the thuds reverberating through the fake canyon between the two buildings.

"Jem!" I called, "Are you in there?" My hand was starting to hurt where I was hitting the door, and I paused for a minute to hold it before I renewed my efforts. I hoped I wasn't too late.

She hadn't answered the phone on the drive. I tried to ring it again. I was sweating, breathing shallowly and pacing up and down the small landing. The phone started ringing again and I pulled the handset from my ear, trying to figure out if I could hear hers ringing in her house. It was a slim chance; who left their phone off silent these days? I pressed my ear to the door, hoping to hear the jingle of the unlikely pop tune that I knew she kept as her ringtone. Nothing. I rang once more, and this time listened for a vibration of a phone on a coffee table or other hard surface.

Still nothing. I stepped back from the door and flung my head back to the sky. I could see the concrete siding and the steel balustrade of the stair raising up another four levels, and the decaying brick of the building opposite. Between them the night sky sat with the overcast pall that always came before a heavy rain. As I kept looking up, running my hands through my hair in exasperation, I saw a pair of eyes appear over the edge of the balustrade, two floors up.

The owner of the eyes had speckled grey hair and less teeth than she should have. A foul-looking flower pattern besmirched the nightgown she had on, and her skin bore the marks of too much sun and not enough care.

"Y'after Jem?" she said. Her voice rasped as she said it, the voice of a woman who'd had her share of cigarettes, and most of somebody else's. I nodded.

"She's not 'ere."

"I can see that," I said. "Where did she go?"

The old lady didn't share my concerns for Jem's whereabouts,

"Oh, she ain't been 'ere for days."

My stomach ran cold. *She hadn't even made it home to change before work.*

How the hell had they gotten to her on the way from my place to hers? I thought. Whoever *they* were must have had an eye on the place from whenever they'd dropped off the note under my door to when they'd seen her leave. The thought sent a thrill through my spine. These people knew who I was. They knew who Jem was. They knew where at least one of us lived… what the fuck was I supposed to do?

I realised that the woman was still watching me from the landing. I must have looked frantic, because she tried to calm me with a "You 'er boyfriend?"

I didn't correct her. "She was with me last night… you said she hadn't been around for a few days? I don't suppose she spoke to you before she left the last time?"

"Nup. She don't talk much. She's always out somewhere though. Little social butterfly, that one." The woman's voice sounded awful, and I was getting agitated just having to listen to her. The rasp was echoing off the concrete in the walls, and I was quickly becoming aware of the fact that I would need to keep my head down if I was to find out who the fuck had kidnapped Jem.

"Okay, thanks," I said. "Guess I'll have to try again later." My voice was wavering, made all the worse for the reverberation between the buildings, and without waiting for the old lady to say anything else I thundered back down the stairs and into my car.

I turned the engine on and roared from Jem's street. I considered somewhere she could have gone that wasn't the worst-case scenario currently screaming through my head. The fact that she'd not been home for several days prior to tonight pointed to her staying somewhere else sometimes, but I had no idea where the hell that could be. She had said that she had work. Maybe I was panicking. Maybe she'd just gone straight there instead of getting changed at home first.

I veered off at a crossroads, cursing whatever late-night traffic there was that was stopping me driving at full speed to the hospital where she worked.

My mind was in overdrive, trying to come up with something that didn't connect directly to the threat I'd received earlier that day. The streetlights were flying by, and I could feel the engine on my piece-of-shit car heating up and wanting to give out on me.

I had noticed she'd been tired the last few times I'd seen her, and she had fallen off the radar a few times prior to this happening. I didn't particularly know what it was she was up to at the time, but that may have had something to do with wherever she was now. I hoped so, and as I thought about it more and more I was able to cling on to that hope. I felt my tensions settle slightly, becoming less worried about Jem and settling more on whoever had left the message. If they *hadn't* taken Jem, then were they after me in particular? Or did they want both of us and they just didn't realise that she wasn't there as well. I cursed myself; I should have tried to check the door at Jem's place to see if she'd had a similar calling card.

I pulled into one of the few visitor car parks at the hospital. The visitor car parks were a long way from anywhere, set away from the hospital proper, probably so that acute care and more urgent patients didn't have to walk so far. Ahead of me lay a blank expanse of long and short-stay carparking, and a complicated series of signs I'd had to navigate to get to the appropriately cordoned-off section.

The hospital itself was a relic from the seventies - far too much of that off-terracotta colouring that somehow slipped into public fashion during that era, and ugly aluminium shutters that weren't so much designed as congealed onto the side. I'm sure that at some point, some architect or other had drawn a beautiful sketch of children playing in the sunshine. Lots of fountains and flowers and things that screamed 'health'. Whatever that vision had been, it had long succumbed to the practicalities of price, technology and time. Pigeon shit and the black corruption from the top of the weep holes and windowsills streaked down the facade, and the enormous air-conditioning unit that sat atop the hulking mass crouched conspicuously. Steam poured from the cooling towers. The whole place was glistening in the reflected moonlight off the puddles in the endless car park, puddles that wavered silkily in the light breeze. I reached the porte-cochere outside the entrance just as the rain started getting heavier. I turned briefly into the open night, then stepped through the automatic doors into the clinical whiteness of the reception area.

The kiosk was staffed by a homely middle-aged woman who kept her hair resolutely dyed a violent shade of red. The glasses on her eyes were exactly the kind of forever-out-of-fashion spectacles favoured by severe librarians and angry customers in department stores. There were a few others in the waiting room, arrayed haphazardly between the small seats and old magazines of doubtful provenance. None of them looked in particularly urgent need of speaking to the receptionist, so I approached her.

For all the glasses and scary hair, she smiled at me warmly and asked, "How can I help you?" in a voice that struck me as at once caring and professional.

"Hi, um. I'm here to see my friend," I said.

"Okay dear, do you know the room number? You can go right in if they're an outpatient." She gestured to the right of the long island desk where she sat; there was a heavy double door that I assumed led to the wing of the hospital for the less-sick people. I realised my mistake immediately and corrected myself.

"Oh, no, sorry. She's an employee, not a patient."

Her demeanour changed subtly. The customer service voice dropped away and she leaned in toward me. "I'm sorry, love. We don't usually allow staff to see people while they're on shift unless they're family. Are you family?"

I considered lying for a moment. We could have passed for brother and sister in a pinch, and there were hints I could drop to her when I saw her that would suggest to her that she should play along. It wasn't likely they'd check my I.D. or anything. I was about to say *Yes, we're family*, when something stopped me. I don't know what it was. We'd worked so hard, Jem and I, together, to make the steps to get out of the world of drudgeries and shams that we'd found ourselves wrapped up in our entire lives. Pat had been taken by it, had got caught in the maelstrom of deceit and substances and filth and moral reprehension that had eventually killed him. Jem and I were on our way out, and somehow I felt that a white lie about this would in some way betray the work we'd done.

"No, I'm not. I'm just a friend," I said, and before the woman behind the counter could speak to reject me, I cut back in, "Look. I'm really sorry and I know it's against policy, but I'm really concerned for her. She and I have been hanging out at my house a lot, and for some reason…" I paused before going on, then took the plunge, "I think she might be in danger."

The layer of false compassion was gone now, and the stern face was in full force, "Young man. I'm not sure who you are, but I think you had best leave. If there are any staff here who are in immediate danger, you should let me know and I'll inform security. We have enough troubles in here looking after the sick people than dealing with people's cruel jokes."

"I'm not joking. Someone left a threatening message at my house that I noticed just after she left. I'm not fucking around. I'm really worried about her." I was stepping back and forth in front of the woman now, dancing on one foot and rubbing my arms anxiously. She regarded me closely through her thick lenses and seemed to make her mind up about something. Her face softened again.

"Okay. What's her name?"

I breathed a sigh of relief. "Jem. Jemima. Jemima Spelling. Tell her it's Pete."

"Okay, Pete. I'll try to hunt her down for you. Please have a seat and I'll get back to you." With that she gestured to a corner of the room.

I sat down, one leg twitching restlessly. I wasn't sure if I should stand waiting too long. I needed to speak to Jem, and to just *see* her and make sure she was okay. It seemed like forever ago that we'd kissed so passionately in the nightclub, and the slight awkwardness after our night between the sheets wasn't even registering in my mind anymore. I found myself almost screaming internally, willing her slender frame to wander through the double doors.

I picked up a magazine and ruffled through. It was some stupid self-help thing, the kind of publication that posits such useful wisdom as *clean your room* and *spend less money than you earn* and acts like it's fucking Kant or something. I flicked through the pages. Most of them were absolute bullshit, as I expected, but I was trying to keep my mind off things. A story on the top ten apps a productive person needed on their phone. Something about the daily routine of some buff gym junkie who had nothing better to do with his time than lift weights. Something about the latest movements in cryptocurrency, blah blah blah.

I tossed it back onto the table and it flipped open to a page. I nearly didn't look, but of course my nervousness loved the excuse to keep moving. I stood up from the chair and moved to the table to flip the magazine back to its front cover when I saw the woman in the picture for the article that it had flipped over to.

It was Kelly. The Aunt of Pat's that had come to the funeral. I picked the rag back up and flipped the page to read the whole article. The further I got in, the wider my eyes got. My leg stopped twitching. I straightened my posture and stared directly down at the page, drinking it in.

Kelly wasn't Pat's aunt at all. She wasn't a relative of his. She worked as –

"Excuse me, sir?" a male voice called across the room, directed at me. I was in shock from the article and didn't respond immediately. I just gawked at the man standing in the double doorway, clipboard, stethoscope and coat identifying him as one of the doctors on duty. I gathered myself, stood and walked over to him.

"We should probably speak somewhere privately," he said to me, and he motioned me through the door. I walked behind him for perhaps forty metres before he turned left into an empty room.

"I heard you were looking for Jemima Spelling?" he said.

"Uh, yes." I said.

"Are you a friend of hers?" he asked.

"Yes. Can I speak to her, please?" I said. The agitation was back, and I felt the faint premonition of something in the base of my chest.

The doctor didn't answer, instead asking, "When did you last see her?"

"This afternoon. She, uh, stayed the night at my house," I said. "Why, what's happening?"

"Well, she didn't turn up for work this evening," he said flatly.

My mind reeled and bile rose in my chest. Somewhere in the background I heard the doctor asking about my comment to the receptionist. *You said she might be in danger* and *do you know what's happened to her* and *should we be concerned.* I didn't answer, just sat slowly onto one of the empty beds in the corner. The sheets crackled as I put my weight down, and my entire world seemed to collapse in as though I was surrounded by cotton.

The doctor put his hand on my shoulder to bring me out of my reverie, "Son, I need you to answer me here. Is she in danger?"

"Don't call me son. She's probably fine."

"But you mentioned to Maureen at reception–" he said.

"She's probably fine. I just haven't seen her. Figured she might be here." My mind was rapidly running through all the places where she might be. It didn't seem likely that she *would* miss work; she'd always been responsible in that regard. I thought she might have been locking herself in her house, but I'd been hollering at her door for quite some time tonight. Where *was* she?

The doctor remained unconvinced, "Pete, if you suspect that

she may be in danger, you have to know that we have a duty of care to inform the authorities of any concerns we have about our staff." He looked at me seriously for a moment. "Do we need to call the authorities?"

I stood up from the bed and pushed past him. "Do what you want. I'm going to go find her." I said to him as I paced back out into the hall.

He didn't chase me on the way back out to the carpark. Probably decided I wasn't worth the effort. As I blew past Maureen at reception and stormed out the automatic doors I already had a cigarette in my mouth which I lit as soon as I was out of the port-cochere. The rain had gotten heavier in the time I'd been inside, so I wrapped my collar up around my ears and stepped out into the wet. I had to curl my fingers around to keep the cigarette lit in the rain and cup the thing to my face as I drew from it.

The walk back to the car seemed to take far longer than necessary, longer than the walk in, and I was drenched by the time I got to it. I was only halfway done with the cigarette, so I stood next to the car to finish it off, pondering what my next move was going to be.

She wasn't at home. She wasn't at work. She'd made a comment before leaving my house that she had a shift that night, so she *knew she had work.*

My mind went back to the slip of paper under the door as I drew down on the damp butt of the cigarette. I flicked it away into the downpour and opened the car door. Once inside, I ditched the soaking jumper and turned the engine over. I grabbed my phone out and checked my messages again. Still nothing from her.

I reversed out of the car park and drove aimlessly into the

night.

* * *

I arrived back at my house at daybreak. I was so exhausted I could barely keep my eyes open. I fumbled the key in the lock and pushed my way back inside. The place was as I'd left it, which was a relief as it meant that whoever had left the note hadn't come back.

I'd gone through every back street, every alley, and every corner I'd ever known Jem to talk about or go to. I didn't expect to see her on the street, but I'd kept driving around anyway. I figured that if I was trying to be everywhere at once then I'd have to see her at some point. It wasn't true. She could have walked out onto any of those streets as soon as I'd exited them. I was out of my brain with worry and I couldn't let myself feel like what I'd been doing might have been pretty much useless. I left the cognitive dissonance bubble in my mind as I kept my search up into the colder and colder hours of the night.

I'd eventually given up. I'd seen the sun rising slowly over the horizon of the slums I'd been driving through and had realised that the longer I kept this up the more likely it would be that she might try to contact me at home or go back to her house.

I walked into the kitchen and brewed myself a coffee that would wake the dead. I wasn't done yet. I considered seeing if I had any more coke stuffed away anywhere to keep myself up, but I knew I'd used it all by the time Pat died, and I hadn't bought more.

The coffee was shocking. I pushed myself into drinking it. Three sugars and a healthy slopping of milk made it almost palatable.

My phone had stayed resolutely silent over the course of the night. I'd barely been able to stop checking it. I found myself angry as I looked at it on my countertop, and directed the fury at whoever had left the message on my doorstep two nights before.

"Fuck you, then, arseholes," I spat toward the phone but at nobody in particular. "You kidnap my friend, I'm going to make sure your drug deals get fucked." With that, I drained the last of my coffee and headed into the spare bedroom, where I found the Spice array still slowly working. I was about a day from having the next batch ready to prepare and the penultimate step in the process was overdue. I picked up the container of ingredients that Jem and I had premixed and poured it carefully into one of the chilled vats. Next, I went back into the kitchen and got the bag of ice from the freezer. I brought it back and put it in the cold wrap. I replaced the lid on everything and moved the hose from the main vat into the chilled one. The two ingredients would do their thing over twelve hours or so; then it would be ready to crystallise.

I went back out to the lounge and grabbed a beer from the fridge on the way. I'd barely cracked it open when despite the coffee I fell into a fitful sleep, haunted by dreams of Jem's final smile before she'd walked away from me.

When I woke up, the sun was going back down again. I staggered out to the bathroom, stripped out of the clothes I'd been wearing for the best part of two days and jumped into the shower. While I was in there, I realised I hadn't checked my phone since getting up. I finished, towelled myself off and walked back out to the lounge room where my nearly-flat phone still lay next to my completely flat beer. I flicked it open and my heart leaped as saw I had a text message.

I rolled it open and scrolled to messages. It wasn't from Jem. It was from a private number, one word:

DON'T.

Chapter 18

For the next twelve hours, after starting the crystallisation process on the batch of Spice, I was in a frenzy. I'd been so concerned with finding out about what had happened to her I'd forgotten about the threat they'd made to me. I realised now that the position I was in was perilous; I had no way of defending myself.

I collected as much food as I could from my kitchen, mainly pasta and non-perishables. I hauled it into a box and hefted it out to the car, then packed the majority of my wardrobe. That took up most of the space in the car once I'd shoved in a suitcase and overnight bag. I packed the toiletries, all my chargers, my laptop and anything else that I thought I'd need into the foreseeable future. I brewed another massive batch of coffee and sat in the Spice room, waiting for the other shoe to drop. Either the crystallisation would finish in time and I'd be able to shoot through in the clear, or whoever was threatening me would arrive first. If it was the latter, I was in big trouble.

It was a long time teetering on the edge of boredom and terror. I kept checking my phone to see if Jem or whoever-the-fuck had messaged me again, and I got nothing. I kept checking to see if the crystallisation was proceeding as it was supposed to and got more and more anxious every time it wasn't done.

Finally I pressed my fingers into the crystallisation tray, and the Spice snapped crisply underneath it. Haphazardly, I pulled a large tupperware container over and snapped off sizeable sections of the contents of the Spice into the container until large shards filled it up.

I rushed out to the car, dumped it into the passenger seat and drove out of the house and around the corner. I drove around for more than an hour, just glad that I'd got away from my house before I realised I had no idea where the *hell* I *was* going to go. What's more, *who were these people?* They seemed to know everything about me. They knew what it was I was doing, and they knew why I was doing it. They knew where I lived. They knew my phone number. They even seemed to be able to read my mind when I'd talked about making more Spice the night before. I'd been alone in my house. How had they known?

I knew of a cheap motel a few miles away. The kind of place you stopped in on while you were going on a fast road trip from one place to another and just needed a bed for the night. Well, some people did, anyway, I'd never exactly been one for long car journeys.

I couldn't pay by credit card; I had to assume that whoever these people were, they'd know as soon as I coughed up a couple of hundred dollars on a traceable transaction.

The motel was even more dilapidated than I remembered. God, this town was a grimy shithole. I used to think that it was just me and my lifestyle that clung like dirt on the side of a shoe to an otherwise clean and wholesome society. The more I saw, though, the more I got the impression that the dirt was everywhere. The attempts to hide it got more effective but it was always there.

Next to the motel was a development that had been abandoned in the housing crash from a few years ago. I remember hearing about it at the time. The whole place was boarded up now, but it had been planned to be a major new housing estate, a construction project to reinvigorate the town's economy. The construction project had fallen through; the company behind it had liquidated and taken the State's investment money with it. Now the place sat there as a reminder of the gullibility of people when money got involved.

The houses themselves were gruesome. Prefabricated bungalows with faux-Grecian columns on porticos too small to make them look real. Thinly applied render that didn't extend to the cheap bricks on the sides, peeling off. Hoarding and scaffold still held up in place next to the gaping holes in the frames where the doors were supposed to go.

I slowed down as I drove past it and turned into the next entrance. The Camelot Motel, it was called. An auspicious name for the kind of place that had thin cutlery covered in rust spots and instant coffee sachets with the consistency and flavour of ground nutmeg. I walked into the reception and waited for someone to show up. The proprietor looked vaguely surprised to see me, as though someone wanting to use her accommodation was a rare inconvenience rather than her whole business model.

"Hourly or daily?" she asked.

"What? Oh– daily. I'm not sure how long I'm staying yet." I said. I realised I hadn't sorted the cash out - it was still in a big wad in my backpack. "Um. Can we start with three nights?"

The woman shrugged. She had the air of someone who had a cigarette dangling from the corner of her mouth even though it wasn't there, and the frizz in her hair must have been left

113

there from whenever it was that perms were in style. "Sure. That's one-eighty. If you wanna stay longer we might have to move your room; can't guarantee the same one'll be available."

I was barely paying attention. I was trying to figure out how I was going to inconspicuously grab two hundred dollars or so from the thousands sitting in my bag without catching this lady's eye. She didn't seem the sort to be able to take it from me, but the whole place struck me as the kind of place where it could be arranged.

I decided to just risk it. The door to the room would have a lock. I shrugged the backpack off my back and up onto the counter and unzipped it. Opening the front pocket, I reached in and started sifting through the notes as inconspicuously as I was able. The woman's face remained impassive, her mouth downturned.

I finally got the money out and handed it to her. She took it silently. I zipped the bag up and took the keys she proffered, turning toward the door. It opened with the cheap tinkle of an old bell held just over the aluminium frame, and I heard her speak.

"You'll want to get that in a bank soon," she said.

"What?" I said.

"I don't know how much you've got in there, but you'll wanna put it in an account. They're setting up cash limits. In a few weeks anywhere you go is going to have to report you for having that much cash on your person." Her eyes betrayed absolutely no concern, but her voice told me she was warning me, not threatening me.

"I –" I didn't know how to respond. "Thanks."

The bell chimed again as the door shut behind me.

There was something about what she'd said that triggered

a memory on the outside edge of my mind. I was trying to make the connection as I hopped back into my still-idling car and headed into the designated carpark just outside the room. I reversed my car in and opened the trunk, grabbing my overnight bag and toiletries and heading inside.

The room was exactly as you would expect from a cheap motel next to an abandoned subdivision. Clean, in a musty sort of way. A series of laminated instructions on a round two-seater table; a towel was laid out on the corner of an absurdly small single bed. There was a small section of ugly brown tiles set into what was probably grey grouting when it was new, and fake timber veneer cupboards forming a small kitchenette. An en-suite completed the picture at the back of the room, along with peeling wallpaper.

I lay on the bed and stared at the ceiling. There was a water stain on it, not dissimilar to the one I had at my house. The more things change, the more they stay the same. I glanced around. There was a large no smoking symbol in the corner. Fuck. I got up and headed outside.

I stood out the front, leaning on my car and slowly sucking down a cigarette. Jem was still missing, and whoever they were they knew far too much about me. There wasn't too much I could do about what they *already* knew, like my address and name and everything. What I could do is try to control how much *more* they could find out.

How the fuck are you going to do that? I asked myself. *You don't even know how they found out about you in the first place. The only thing they don't know right now is where you are, and that's assuming they didn't somehow tail you here.*

I didn't think that was likely, if I was honest, but once again I found myself flicking Pat's lighter against my leg.

Pat, I thought, and I remembered the article I'd seen about Kelly in the hospital. At the funeral, she'd told us that she was Pat's long-lost aunt, but something hadn't felt right about it. She hadn't seemed as upset as a family member would be. It was almost like she'd seen the situation play out a thousand times before.

The article I'd seen had answered so many questions. I knew Pat wouldn't have kept something like that from me. Well, it turned out that he hadn't. Kelly was a support worker. More specifically, she was a case worker for the local council that had set up a new program whereby people without support networks could come in and get helped with their problems. It didn't matter what those problems were, whether they were relationships, violence in the home, mental illness... or drugs.

Pat didn't have a secret aunt. He had a secret case worker. He'd known he had a problem and had found out about this program of Kelly's, and he'd signed himself up. He'd been more aware of his addiction than any of us had been, and he'd stepped in and given himself an intervention before Jem or I had even known he had a problem.

Fucking Pat. He had been trying to do what I was trying to do now. My idea of becoming a Spice trader to get out of this was his, and it had cost him his life. Just a stupid mistake from one night of getting fucked up with me.

The lighter was in my hands, and I flicked the butt of the cigarette into the steel box ashtray as I walked back inside.

I pulled the box of Spice out of my bag and looked at it. I ripped off the lid and stalked over to the kitchenette. There was nothing notable I'd be able to break the stuff up with. I would have preferred a blender or at very least a mortar and pestle, but all I had was a thin fork or a teaspoon or two. I grabbed a coffee mug. It was the only thing in the kitchenette sturdy enough to break up the Spice. With a sort of mindless determination, I started pushing and twisting the mug into the Tupperware container. I gave it no quarter. Even as my arm grew weary and started to ache, I kept pushing and twisting into it. My shoulder burned, and I started sweating. The coffee mug slipped from my grasp several times, as did the Tupperware container, but finally I had the entire batch ground down to a fine powder.

It was after midnight. Exhausted, I once again flopped onto the bed, stared at the water stain on the ceiling, and tried not to think about what had happened to my dead friend, or what was happening to my friend who was still alive. A slow, creeping dread came over me. Jem was stuck somewhere, and I couldn't find her. Someone, or many someones, were after me, and I didn't know how, or why. As far as I knew, it wasn't safe to go home. I wasn't safe to use my bank cards. In a few weeks, I wouldn't be safe to use cash. There was only a little while that I'd be safe to stay here. The hopeless futility of the situation bore down on me in the darkness of that hotel room, and the cold of the night crept in and settled on my chest like the demon of my night terrors.

Chapter 19

When my phone went off at half past four in the morning, I jerked awake from a sleep I didn't know I'd fallen into and lunged for the glowing rectangle in the darkness. The vibration had thrown it off the edge of the cheap bedside desk, and I slid myself out of bed and half onto the floor as I struggled to read the screen and hit the answer button.

"H'lo?" I mumbled.

"Pete?"

I jerked the rest of my body to the floor and pulled the bedsheet away from me. I sat bolt upright and held the phone to my ear. The sleep had flown out of my head as fast as her voice had hit my brain.

"Jem? Where are you? Where have you been? Are you okay? What's happening?"

"You sent me... a lotta messages, Pete. Whass goin' on? You tryna scare me?" She sounded drunk. Or no, not drunk. Something else. Her voice was slurred and she was speaking super slowly. It was like she was drugged.

They had her.

"Where are you, Petey? Haha. Petey," she giggled on the other end of the line, a drawn out, gurgling sound that made me sick to hear.

If she'd been drugged and tricked into calling me, they'd be listening in. "I can't tell you where I am. Can you tell me where you are?"

I heard yells in the background. They sounded like someone hopped up on too much meth would sound. Brash and angry, and like the world was out to get them.

"Jem. Where are you? I'm coming to find you." There were a few more mumbling incoherent sounds and then the phone shut off.

I held the phone to my ear a little longer, the dial tone pounding through my skull. She'd caught a moment and found a way to call me, and I couldn't even get any useful information out of her before she'd been pulled away. I felt an impotent rage well up within me as I tried to figure out where she'd been taken.

I got up from where I'd wrapped myself in the blanket while I'd been talking to Jem. It was pitch dark in the room, and I'd pulled the entirety of the bedclothes off the bed during the short conversation. They'd ended up tangled in between my legs and I fumbled to get out of them in the dark. I reached up to the bedside table and turned on the light, then searched through the apartment to try and find where I'd left the jeans I'd torn off when I'd tried to get to sleep.

I had a dry feeling in my mouth, and I could hear nothing outside the thudding permeating my body from inside my ribcage. The lamplight threw slick shadows over the aging wallpaper, and the pile of clothes I'd left in the corner loomed at me. Pulling on a T shirt and a jumper, I found the key to the room. I was out the door and in my car before I started thinking straight. Jemima was drugged up in some room somewhere and everything else faded into oblivion in the face of that one simple fact.

I sat in the driver's seat, and I felt my posture crumple. The initial adrenaline shock of having heard Jem's voice had worn off. It was still the middle of the night, and I had not the slightest clue as to where Jem might be holed up. If she was in a drug dealer's house, who knew where the hell she was? That could be anywhere. I was cooking up Spice in my spare bedroom but from the outside my house seemed as unobtrusive and boring as any other on the street. How was I supposed to find her at all?

I was filled with a feeling of impotence and futility, and in that moment I knew I was never going to find her. I thought about calling the police. I'd go into the station that night. I'd tell them everything - the Spice trading. The threats. The phone messages. The way Jem had suddenly disappeared.

No. Wait. She hadn't *suddenly* disappeared, had she? She'd had days of being uncontactable every now and then since Pat's death. What would the police even say? That a grown woman was uncontactable? Wasn't that completely within her rights? And anyway, why were you calling her so often? Were you stalking her? What was your relationship? Oh, you slept together just prior to her not contacting you?

I could see the whole line of questioning spiraling out of my control in my mind, and I saw that nothing I was going to say could help. I bet the police could have easily figured out where she was though. Hell, they could trace your credit cards and stuff so all you'd need to do was make a purchase–

Wait a minute.

The comment that the woman had made at the reception just before she'd leased me the room – *In a few weeks anywhere you go is going to have to report you for having that much cash on your person.* That had stuck in my mind before, and I wondered why it was bouncing around the edge of my recognition. I'd *known* it was important, but I couldn't figure out what cash had to do with anything. It wasn't the new law about cash holdings that had tripped me up; it had been the connection to something I'd heard not long ago. Crazy Jake had gotten it right.

You use cash and they'll arrest you! It's gonna be illegal, dude! They'll use your phone to track your every move.

My gut roiled. The air seemed to go out of my lungs. A few days before the message arrived at my door, I'd heard that the new laws about cell phone data retention had been made legal.

My mind was whirring again now, and I sat buckled into the front seat of my car. The 'DON'T' message I'd received on my phone hadn't been a *second* warning about not cooking Spice anymore, it had been a response to me telling the empty room in my house that I was going after the drug traffickers. They'd been listening to what my phone had recorded me saying.

They'd been able to figure out my address. They'd been able to slip a note under my door at some point. A note I hadn't even noticed. I hadn't heard anyone walk up to my house, and I would have because the stairs out the front creaked terribly whenever I did. They'd *waited until I wasn't home.*

I stared at the phone in my hand. I wasn't going to be able to escape this forever. I wasn't even going to be able to escape it for more than a few hours. They, quite literally, had my number. If I threw my phone away, it could only possibly last another week or two until the cash restriction laws came in, and I'd be stuck unable to pay for anything lest they find me.

I remember Pat saying that Spice wasn't illegal. It was a brand-new drug that had no side effects and didn't have any problems with it, but for some reason I don't think the finer points of its effects really made much of a difference. Like one of us had assumed, the powers that be wouldn't just accept that; they'd see this new drug as a new threat the same way meth had been in the 90s, and the way that LSD had been before that. I was nothing but a new and different brand of felon, waiting to be rounded up and locked in a cage. The longer I considered it, the more it grew in my mind until it was an all-encompassing truth that took away everything else. It took away Jem, it took away Pat, it took away everything and left its mark in my mind like a glowing neon distraction.

They were after me, but that didn't make sense.

Why were the *police* after me?

Chapter 20

The Camelot Motel was no longer a safe place for me to be. I had to assume that it never had been, and that the cops had known of my whereabouts the moment I'd arrived. Why they hadn't arrived yet I didn't know, but I didn't have time to question it.

For the second time in as many days, I found myself bursting through a door that had represented safety and taking stock of which belongings to bring with me. I looked again at my phone: it was my potential lifeline for Jem, wherever she was. I found it hard to believe that the cops had her now; it would have been too easy to bring me in. She must have got involved the wrong way with one of her dealers or something. I'd have to figure that out later.

I ripped the back out of the phone. I took the sim and the battery out and threw them along with the phone into the tiny bathroom sink. I pulled the courtesy shampoo bottle out of the shower recess and yanked at the top. It didn't budge initially - it was too slippery, but I tried three or four more times until it popped out into my hand. I poured it all over the collection of pieces in the sink, then wrenched the hot tap on, drenching the lot of them. I had no idea if the soap would make it less salvageable, but I figured it couldn't hurt.

I collected my things again. As I pulled the Spice container towards myself, I thought better of taking the whole mess with me. I pulled a bunch of sandwich bags out of the kitchenette and poured the Spice into it. Next, I put one of them in each of the pockets of my trousers, and the rest into the front pocket of my hoodie. The Tupperware was useless to me now, so I rinsed it out and threw it into the bin.

Moving quickly, I separated the cash out of my backpack into another pocket, so it was the only thing in there. I'd be able to get to it quickly. I stuffed my clothes into the overnight bag. I pounded out of the room, leaving the door open.

I loaded the bags into the passenger seat of my car, then headed to the back. I pulled open the trunk and rummaged around in the left-hand side of it until I found the small toolkit I kept in there for emergencies. I opened it and pulled out a Philips-head screwdriver.

I stooped down and began prying off the number plates. They were grimy and soaked with detritus from the recent rains, but they weren't too hard to remove. Once I had the rear plate off, I left it on the ground and did the same thing at the front of the car. With both of them gone, I grabbed them and stashed them in the industrial bin down the side of the motel. My car now anonymous, I cracked the front door, cast my eyes around the plaza of the motel to see if anyone had seen me, jumped in and started the ignition.

The car burbled to life, and it took every millimeter of my self-control not to slam it into reverse and get out of the car park as fast as I could. To be honest, that kind of behaviour probably wasn't uncommon at the 'hourly-or-nightly' Camelot Motel, but I thought it better to not risk attracting the attention of the other guests. I pulled out of the parking spot and turned out of the plaza. I had begun to rack my brain as to where I could go when I drove past the abandoned lot. I saw a series of headlights flying past me toward the motel at great speed and I panicked. I swung the still-accelerating car into the lot, a small squeak coming from the back wheels and the worn-out shock absorbers bedding down to take the inertia. I maneuvered through the open gate into the ghost town. It wasn't a great hiding place but it was the only one I could think of at short notice. At least the houses would be a good place to hide, hopefully.

I searched frantically for a place to hide the car. Parking it in one of the open carports would be too conspicuous; it would get found pretty much straight away. I had to find a place with a *garage,* where I could close a door behind me.

Before too long, I found one. I pulled up and left the car idling as I walked to the handle and pulled it. It flexed underneath my pull, but it didn't budge upward. Locked. The headlights illuminated the keyhole - it wouldn't be any use, I couldn't pick locks.

I swore softly, then panicked as I realised that if I could see from my headlamps, then the convoy that had just pulled up at the motel would be able to as well. Across the clear night air, I heard raised voices from several hundred metres away. It seemed as though they'd found the empty room, and they weren't happy about it. I could see them crowded around from my vantage point in the driveway - the motel was only a few hundred metres away as the crow flies. The cars were all black and there were four of them that I could see, their headlamps throwing my motel room into stark relief against the black of the rest of the night.

I scrambled back to the car door and switched the headlamps

off as quickly as I could and looked back up at the hotel. They were still milling around, and I couldn't see any of the people clearly enough to know what they were doing or what they'd do next.

I decided to see if I could break a window to get around and unlock the garage door from the inside. The night was overcast and my eyes hadn't adjusted to the darkness yet, but I headed quickly to the left of the garage toward the house proper. The front door sat black and solid in front of me - no luck there. I scrambled around in the scrubby foliage that had grown in place of a lawn, trying to find a heavy object of some sort. A brick or a rock would do. There was a very slight breeze, and every now and then I'd hear a shout of something coming from the direction of the motel. *Come on, come on.* I was begging for something heavy enough to find, and then I cracked my knuckles on it. A concrete block.

I sank next to it and pulled my hoodie off. I took the two sandwich bags of spice I had in the hoodie and stuffed them into the pockets of my trousers. I wrapped the hoodie around the top part of my right arm and hand. I lifted the brick into my right hand with my left and made my way to the window.

The wrapping the hand trick was something I'd heard somewhere once, probably while shitfaced at some point. Supposedly it made it less likely you'd slice an artery when you broke the window. I didn't know. Of all the experiences I'd had in my life, breaking a window to get away from the cops hadn't been one of them.

I breathed in, then out again, trying to ignore the tremors. *Okay,* I thought. *Here goes.* I planted my feet and swung violently from the hip, almost wrenching my arm from its socket as the block arced up around my hand and collided with the glazing.

The glass calved into four enormous sheets, and shattered into crystalline mist at the same moment. The largest pieces collapsed on either side of the frame, one of them striking my head on the way through. They fell to the ground and annihilated themselves on the bare concrete, bursting into sharp icicles at my feet. The smaller sections flew everywhere and lodged themselves in my skin and my clothes and my hair. I had closed my eyes instinctively, and I was glad of it.

This all happened in a moment, and it released a shearing, wrenching cacophony that could have woken the dead. I practically *saw* the soundwave scream out into the night. Saw it rush down the street and assault the ears of the occupants of the four cars currently searching for me in the hotel room my phone had led them to.

Within a couple of seconds, I heard an engine rev, then another and another. The time left for me to try discretion was over.

I took a running leap into the empty window frame, barely avoiding the leftover pieces of window that remained held in by the adhesive around the edges. My shoes crunched on the shards as I sprinted to the garage door. It was pitch black, and I instinctively reached for my phone's flashlight before I remembered it wasn't there. I fumbled blindly around the walls, smacking my shoulder as I hit the edge of the garage door. I moved my hands around until I felt the rail that held the latch, and traced it to the centre, where the latch was. I breathed – it was a sigh of relief as I realised it was the same latch as Pat had had at his house. It allowed a manual override to the locking mechanism from the inside. I twisted it and threw the door up, peering into the darkness at the motel. The police, or whoever they were, were still organising their way into the cars but they wouldn't be far away. I got into my still-idling car and drove it into the garage. I turned the engine off then fumbled my way into the backpack I'd left on the seat. I pulled it out, then got out of the car and ran from the garage, stopping only to slam the door down.

I was thinking as fast as I could in the situation, and I thought the best way to minimise the trouble I might find myself in would be to spread the evidence around. I didn't want to be caught with the car, the phone, the cash, *and* the drugs on me all at once. That would make my case very hard to plea. If I was caught with nothing, but things happened to turn up around me? Well… maybe I could argue that it was all a coincidence. It still wasn't likely, but it was the best my mind could come up with in the panic.

Holding the wad of cash in one hand, I patted my pockets to make sure the Spice was still there. I ran, sprinting at full pelt for maybe a hundred metres, but then the cigarettes and lack of exercise got to me and I was forced to slow down. Gasping for air, I slowed to a light jog. I paused at a letterbox and lifted the cheap metal lid. I shoved the money in there, then kept moving, this time looking for a house that I'd be able to break into quietly and without fuss. The police cars had made it into the street, and I could see the edges of headlights reflecting off the street signs around the ghost neighbourhood.

I only had a few seconds to find something. I stopped running, and coughed into my hand as I stooped over.

No way they're finding me out here, I said to myself. Looking around, I saw that I had stumbled onto a street that was less completed than others. Instead of doors and windows installed with no fixtures inside, these ones had gaping holes that were still hidden with scaffolding. One or two of them had no roofing, just exposed timber frames that were starting to show signs of rot.

I chose one that had a roof on it and a series of torn translucent sheets taped over the windows. It was surrounded by the high fences that they use at construction sites to keep kids out. I leaped up and grabbed at the holes in the chicken wire with my fingers, then hoisted myself up and over the top.

A terrible ripping sound came from my trousers and I had to stifle a cry of pain when I thundered into the ground. I'd done something to my leg– it must have got caught at the top of the fence. When I looked up I saw the problem; the top of the fence was covered in razor wire. Just how security conscious *were* they about this estate? My leg burned when I stood up and tried to put weight on it, so I half-limped, half-hobbled into the house. This one didn't have a front door, and I left a bloody shoe print in the dust as I crossed the threshold. I staggered through the house and found a room that didn't have a window that connected directly outside. There were pipes coming through the floor; it was probably going to end up being someone's bathroom or something. Through the empty doorway I could see the dirt-stained plastic sheets that blocked a direct view to the outside. I lowered myself to the floor, grunting with pain, such that I could still see the window through the doorway.

I leaned my back against the wall, wheezing quietly. The sheet to the outside was dark, punctuated only by the occasional glaring reflection of a torch. It seemed as though they'd abandoned their vehicles; I could no longer hear them, but I could hear voices. If I was listening carefully, I would have been able to hear exactly what the search team was saying, but I knew the specifics didn't really matter. I ran my hand down my leg and gasped slightly as I felt the gash I'd given myself when I'd jumped the fence. It had ripped through my trousers like they were paper, not polycotton, and the fabric was slick with blood. The razor wire had snagged against my skin and torn an enormous chunk out of my thigh. It was streaming with blood.

I held myself very still, willing myself to breathe more quietly as I tried to find any other injuries I'd sustained. Everything hurt, but it was mainly bruising and I didn't think there was much in the way of actual lacerations aside from my leg. I was losing a lot of blood. I looked back toward the window. I could see a shining trail showing the history of my path into the room in the torchlight outside.

I'd started bleeding outside on the dirt, at least. It would mean that there wasn't any slick patch on the concrete to worry about that might catch someone's eye. What I really wanted to do right now was to get rid of the Spice that was filling up all my pockets. The money was gone, as was the car. I'd flushed my phone with soap *and* water in that hotel room. The only thing that the police had to tie me to the drugs now were the drugs themselves. I found myself wishing that the house had been more complete; that way I could have dumped it in the toilet or flushed it down the sink. Something so I wouldn't get caught with it on my person. As it was, I only had the services penetrations in the concrete floor, and I didn't have anything to take the caps off with.

If I was caught, I was screwed either way, but at least I'd be able to try to reduce my punishment if I didn't have Spice on me. Though if they'd been recording audio from my phone, they'd probably have enough to mark me as a dealer and put me away.

Something about this didn't make sense though. *I'm not dealing illegal drugs,* I thought. Why are the police hunting me down?

I held my right hand against my thigh, trying in vain to stem the blood loss, then reached toward the pocket in my jeans. I felt the edge of the bag of Spice and pulled it out, but something made me stop before it left my pocket. It felt too light. Fumbling, I felt carefully around the edges of the packet, keeping it carefully in my pocket, hoping I wouldn't find the slit in the bag I already knew must be there. Sure enough, there it was. A tear big enough to put your thumb through, matched with a pair of cuts from the outside of my trousers to the pocket lining. The stuff was leaking out, and my pocket felt like it was filled with a fine silica sand. Not only that but it had got through the pocket itself, and my right leg was covered not only in blood, but was gritty where the Spice had adhered to my leg hairs, blood, and sweat.

I pulled my hand out. My fingers were coated with a layer of the stuff, mixing with the rest of the grime I'd accumulated while I'd fled. I resisted the urge to lick my fingers; the last thing I wanted to do was end up high by accident. My mind raced as I tried to figure out a way to dispose of the stuff now that it was everywhere, but a small corner of my mind knew it was hopeless. My blood would tell the story of where I'd gone if I tried to go anywhere to get rid of it, and the split in the bag had ruined my chance of getting away without them knowing I was in possession of it.

I had to hope that they wouldn't notice where I'd gone. That they'd assumed I'd run out of the estate or gone somewhere that had nothing to do with the broken window they'd heard. If I could just wait it out, maybe I could get home and start to figure out some way of starting to live my life as a fugitive.

The torches flashed at the window sheet again, and I saw the small pools of blood on the floor give off a flash of reflection. They weren't looking directly into the house yet, but it seemed like only a matter of time. I rubbed the fingers on my right hand against my thumb, feeling the rasp of the Spice between the pads and the slick of my own blood. I couldn't get rid of it. They'd be able to pick up the trace amount that would get absorbed into my skin, and then they'd just have to go through my clothes to find the crystals themselves.

"Fuck," I breathed. I could hear the voices murmuring outside, and underneath it the revving of a single engine, growing nearer and farther away as it roamed the streets. Looking out at the sheeting on the windows was freaking me out. I pulled myself across the floor of the unfinished bathroom and hid next to the door, where I could see the patterns of light flashing across the opposite wall. A slick black mark showed the bloody trail where I'd pulled myself along, shimmering darkly.

The sound of the vehicle grew louder, revving wildly as it headed in my direction. It slowed down and I heard someone yell, "Check every fucking house! He's hiding here somewhere!"

Something indistinguishable followed, a susurration that slipped perfectly into the idling sound of the car. The first voice must have been the driver, who I heard yell back.

"Open the boot. There's a pair of bolt cutters."

More voices. *They're coming through the fence.* I was completely boxed in. If I fled now they'd see me; there was no way of knowing how many policemen were outside. There must have been at least three out the front. I wondered if there was a back door that I could get to.

The car drove off, and I could hear the chain link fence getting cut with the bolt cutters. It was now or never. I pushed against the ground with my hands, alarmed at how soaked the ground and my trousers had become with the blood seeping from my right leg. I dizzied as I stood up; if it hadn't already been dark I would have been doused in blackness as the blood rushed from my head. I was feeling weak, and I could only gingerly put any weight on my injured leg. I hobbled to the main living room where I could hear a pair of voices mumbling through the regular sharp snaps the boltcutters made against the fence.

I headed toward the back door. They were shining one light directly through the tattered sheet and it cast a diffuse opalescent light across the floor.

"Hurry up," I heard a particularly rough voice say. "I think I saw something move in there."

"Don't you think I'm fucking trying?" came the response. This one was younger, and didn't sound like it had been subjected to a lifetime of strong cigarettes. It grunted with each snap of the bolt cutters.

The backyard was surrounded by the fencing as well, and I was dizzy from the blood loss. There was no way I'd be able to climb it again. I tried to think about any other options I might have for running away but I came up dry.

There was a small plank of wood sitting next to the back door. It was covered in concrete on one side. It must have been what they used to set the concrete slab. I bent down and picked it up, just as I heard footsteps echo through the empty house. I stood next to the back door on the outside of the house, holding the concrete and timber plank like a cricket bat.

"Look at this," the rough voice said, and the torchlight shrank back from the doorway. *Holy shit, they were inside,* I thought.

My breath came in ragged gasps that I struggled to keep silent, my hands were slick with as much sweat as blood as I waited, poised.

"He's here. And he's hurt." the other voice said. They must have seen my footprint in the door, or the trail of blood. I held myself steady, willing my tiring arms to stay up, ready to spring. I heard the footsteps recede as they followed my trail to the bathroom, and then increase in volume again to follow it out.

Here it goes, I thought. In the back of my mind I realised they weren't calling for backup, that with me planning to smack them with a concrete-covered stick I'd go from drug dealer to assaulting a police officer, and that the latter would be far worse for me. On the other hand, they had made it clear that they were coming after me and I had to defend myself.

The first one through the door was the younger one. His torchlight led him through, and the beam concentrated into a smaller and smaller region in the dusty night air as he approached. The torch appeared, then his arm, then his face just behind it.

I swung my makeshift bat at the man, but the angle I was standing at wasn't very useful for an attack, and the swing was slow and weak. Halfway through the bat's arc, I saw him turn and shoot his free hand out toward the weapon. He caught it easily and used his leverage to wrench it and my arm down at a crippling angle. I cried out in pain as he twisted violently, trying to move my body with him as the angle became more and more unnatural.

With the hand holding the torch, he punched me in the jaw, and I collapsed onto the ground. The second officer came through the door after the first had dealt with me, but I didn't get to see what he looked like because I was dazed, and the flashlight was shone directly into my eyes. The younger guy pinned me down and held me on the ground, resting a hand on my injured right leg.

Again I noticed nobody was calling for backup as the second guy frisked me. He found the Spice bags in my left pockets almost immediately but didn't venture to the right pocket. I looked down and could see why. My entire right side was covered in shiny liquid darkness, the stain spreading from my leg into a pool that was growing onto the concrete path beside me. I felt a sudden urge to vomit and bit it back.

"Looks like someone's had a rough night," the gravelly voice of the older man stuttered through the torchlight and I strained again to see him in detail. I could only see the silhouette of a lean figure with a long beard and a heavy jacket.

I said nothing. Anything I said at this point was going to incriminate me.

"Come on, bud. We found the product on you. You know we've been after you. You *had* to know this was coming after you threatened us," he said. The low growl was almost conciliatory, as though he was explaining the facts of nature to a two-year-old.

"When did I threaten the police?" I choked. My leg was burning where the younger guy had his foot on it; he wasn't putting any pressure on it, but he was making sure I wasn't able to move without causing me extreme pain. I was gasping just from the effort of asking the question. I couldn't seem to get enough air into my lungs, even though I was breathing in as deeply as I could.

The growl turned into laughter and I realised I'd made a mistake. I knew something had been off with my thought process when I had assumed the police had been after me for trading Spice. I had been right. The stuff wasn't illegal. They didn't give a shit at all, and Jem's disappearance and my flight hadn't been to escape the police at all.

"You're not cops, are you?" I breathed.

The young guy laughed and shook his head, then stamped down hard on my thigh. A bolt of pain shot through me so powerful that I thought I was going to pass out. I tried to roll my body to the right to escape but he grabbed me and pushed me back onto my back and slapped me in the face.

"Oh good, we've got an idiot," the older man said, then made a motion with his hand. The boot twisted into my thigh once more and I grimaced. "Of course we're not the cops, you little dickweed. Now, where's your girlfriend?" With that he knelt next to me and pulled a bowie knife from his belt. I panicked and tried to crawl away but couldn't without causing myself more pain. The kneeling man moved toward me and for the first time his face fell into the torchlight.

He was gaunt, with the hollow eyes of a long-time addict. The pupils were dilated and black as pits. Long, fierce scars ran down the left side of his face down to his neckline, and what wasn't marked by scar tissue was impossibly wrinkled. His beard was mostly white with only a few flecks of black left in it, and his head was shaved and covered with linework tattoos. He was grinning sadistically as he moved the knife slowly from my throat to my groin and back again, putting just enough pressure on it for the razor-sharp edge to rasp against the fabric of my hoodie.

"Tell you how this is gonna go, you little fucker. I'm going to ask you again, and you're going to tell me. Because until we've made it clear to both of you that you're not going to be moving in on us with your Spice *shit*," he spat the words and flecks of

136

saliva hit me on the face, "your lives are on thin fucking ice. So I'm going to ask you one more time, and you're going to tell me straight away. *Where the fuck is your little bitch of a girlfriend?"*

"She's with you!" I screamed, thrashing around, "You got to her long before I did! I thought she'd been picked up by the cops! I thought it was you!" I couldn't stop myself moving. Breathing was laboured, even after a burst as short as that. I realised I was rambling and not making a lot of sense, but I couldn't seem to stop myself. Terror had gripped me and it felt harder and harder to get enough air. I was panicked and trying to wrangle my way from the grasp of the two thugs. They weren't impressed. Quick as a snake, the older man clasped my jaw in his hand and pried it apart with a wiry strength I didn't think someone so thin could possess. He put the tip of the blade inside my cheek and pressed into it firmly. I tasted blood in the back of my throat and held very still. The foot stamped down on my injured leg and twisted slowly. Stars of pain were floating in my eyes. He pulled the knife back out. I turned my head and spat a gob of blood and saliva into the ground.

"Don't *fucking* hide her from us!"

"How the hell were you able to trace me?" I blurted and got a powerful slap across the face. The gravelly laugh again.

"What, you think that we can't get a mole into a police unit to trace metadata? Don't play fucking coy with me. I'm not going to ask again. *Where is she?"*

Struggling to hold on to consciousness through the pain, my mind reeled. *They don't know where Jem is. They were tracing my phone, but for some reason couldn't get a lead on Jem. Which means that whatever has happened to her has had nothing to do with this. They know I'm the cook, but she's the distributor, and they don't want either of us in the picture anymore.* Stars were bursting behind my eyelids as the pain increased. It felt like I was going to lose consciousness.

A tiny moment of clarity came through the abyss of the dark that threatened to overwhelm me. In a moment, I saw through what had been happening with Jem after Pat's death. I knew what she was doing, even if I didn't know where she was. The realisation made me want to scream, but the bearded man still had a knife to my throat.

"I *don't know where she is!*" I yelled, "*I fucking swear. I haven't seen or heard from her in days.*"

That wasn't true, and I knew it. She'd called me earlier that night.

The younger guy turned to the bearded one. "I dunno… it sounds like he's telling the truth." The two of them looked at each other, and in that moment both relaxed their grip on me. The knife at my throat lost its pressure, and the foot on my leg came completely off.

I took the opportunity. I kicked the young one's leg out from under him and he collapsed on the ground, then I commando rolled to the left and knocked the feet out from the older man. I stood up, swinging my fists at where I expected the old guy to stand up. One of them connected with his jaw, and I turned to run as he fell back. The two of them were scrambling over each other to get back at me, which gave me an opportunity to turn tail and run.

I scrambled back into the house and hobbled through, following the walls with my left hand in the pitch blackness. My leg was screaming and my breath was short. In the darkness I watched stars exploding into my vision. I passed the bloody foot mark I'd left at the front door and flew into the front yard.

I could see the hole in the fence and a pair of bolt cutters they'd used to make it strewn on the ground. I made a break for it, gasping for air and slowing down substantially as I neared the fence that demarcated the front yard. The two men were behind me but seemed as though they'd stopped the chase. I hobbled through the hole and limped lamely out and down the pebblecrete driveway.

The two men caught up with me almost immediately. I felt a blow on the back of my head and collapsed forward onto the bitumen roadway. I felt a new barrage of cuts and scrapes hit me as I skidded along the ground, and then the younger one was on me. He pinned me down, squatting on my prostrate form and striking me with blow after blow. White spots exploded in my vision again. All thought fled from me as my world was overtaken by the rhythmic thudding of the fists on my skull.

When the beating was done, I opened my eyes. The night sky was overcast, but the edges of my vision were going even darker. The form of the clouds lost shape.

The two men were standing over me, and a third joined them from the other side.

"He's done for," the third said.

"Yeah," came the growl, "and it sounds like the girl won't be a problem either."

The third hesitated. I lay impassive on the ground, staring up at the sky. A chill had overtaken my body and a sense of floating peace was in my mind.

"What do you need, boss?" the young man said, staring down at me. "Do we finish him off?"

I was aware of the conversation in an abstract way. I knew they were talking about me, but it didn't seem to matter that they were discussing my imminent demise.

The third man, the boss, thought for a moment and then answered, "No. We don't need a murder investigation on our backs, especially with the new surveillance rules," he looked at me. "Teach him his lesson. Then leave him." with that, he turned and walked into the growing darkness at the edge of my vision.

The bearded dealer knelt beside me again. This time when he gripped my jaw I didn't protest. He pulled the knife from his side and inserted it into my mouth again. I had a vague feeling of impending horror, but the pain felt like it was coming from far away as he ripped the knife swiftly through the side of my mouth, sawing roughly up toward my ears. I gurgled a scream as he turned the knife and cut the other half of the Chelsea smile. Blood poured into the back of my throat, and I swallowed in an attempt to be able to continue to breathe. A part of my mind reminded me to turn my head to the side. I felt the flap of my cheek hit the bitumen, and I sobbed hopelessly on the ground.

There was a conversation happening. I could hear the young man talking to someone, but I was past caring who. The ash grey of the road blended with the deep blue of the night sky and turned seamlessly into the void consuming my wakeful mind.

Something small hit me on the chest and bounced off, and I could feel dirt rubbing into my teeth through my lacerated cheek as I slipped into the quiet darkness.

Chapter 21

The room was white. That was the first thing I noticed. There were no details that I could reasonably discern. It was the opposite of my last memory. The whiteness slowly granulated into more detail, instead of the blackness that had previously enveloped my world. A small TV screen. A series of monochrome displays with numbers rising and falling. Soft, machine-like beeps. A stench of powerful bleaches and sterile plastics.

The pain was there, but it was only mild. I tried to move my leg but it was held in place, and the effort of trying to move it exhausted me. My arms were leaden and covered with cannulas and wristbands. There was a clipboard at the end of the bed, and several bags of solutions being drip-fed into me.

The blackness returned. I welcomed it.

This process must have happened several times over many days. Each time was a little longer, and I noticed more each time. I woke over and over, and I felt a little stronger, a little realer, a little more human.

Eventually I had enough strength to lift my hands again. When I saw my left arm I felt a stabbing sense of shock. Myriad colours from pale yellow to black and blue and red mottled my skin, and there were tubes pouring out from needles held in my veins. I reached up to touch my cheeks.

I must have looked horrific. I felt a series of stitches running from the corner of my lips to the back of my cheek where the knife would have met my jaw bone. The crackled, itchy feeling of a huge amount of scar tissue had lodged itself in between the stitching and I could practically feel my skin trying to sew itself back together. I tried to reach inside my mouth but I couldn't open it far without it hurting. I steeled myself against the pain, and placed my finger next to my mouth, ready to force it open, when a nurse walked in.

He had red hair and a face mask on, and a set of the most astonishingly blue eyes I'd ever seen. He wasn't tall, and he had the gait of a man who had been doing this for years and had an easy familiarity with patients.

"I wouldn't do that if I were you," he said as I made my move to shove my fingers in my mouth. "Too much movement and you'll split it all over again, and you don't have much blood left to lose."

I stopped, then tried to ask what happened, but my mouth was practically wired shut, so it came out as "Wha' 'appen?"

"I should be asking *you* that. Somebody found you and placed an emergency call on your own phone, then left you at the scene. You had a severe laceration on your leg which didn't look deliberate, sliced open cheeks that definitely were, a bruised jaw, a black eye, cuts, scrapes, bruises all over your body. The cuts had mud and bitumen and gravel ground into them, and at least some of it was deliberate. You were covered in blood, gore and some sort of crystalline stuff we sent off to the lab for testing. We got to you in just in time; there was a concern that you were brain dead. You're lucky to be alive."

Lucky, I thought. The mention of the injuries had brought

back with it a shock of violent memories from the night. Something stuck on the edge of my mind from what the nurse had said but I was still dazed so I couldn't figure it out. My body ached, and I was still coming to terms with what had happened.

I asked for a mirror, and the red-haired man brought one over and held it up for me to see myself. The bruising I'd seen on my body was nothing to what was on my face. My right side had a huge blemish on the base of the jawline and the remains of a shining black eye. It was my cheeks, however, where the true horror lay.

The scabs weren't between the stitches as I had thought; it had grown through them, and over them and around them. The red pustulated mass was an ugly streak running up my jaw line in the centre of a black bruise that took up almost my entire face. I looked silently at the image of myself, then nodded stoically to get the mirror taken away.

The nurse moved around my bedside a bit and took several readings, noting them onto the clipboard. I couldn't find out what they meant, but he seemed satisfied enough.

My life had been spared, and I didn't know why. I vaguely recalled the comment about the difficulty of having to deal with a murder investigation if they had killed me. If that was the case, I had the tracking technology to thank for saving my life, as well as being responsible for the assault in the first place. The fact that they had infiltrated the local police force to the extent that they could track someone like me using my metadata *purely to give me a warning* terrified me.

They still had no idea what had happened to Jem though, and I had to find her before anything else happened to her.

"'Ow long 'm I stug in 'ere?" I asked the nurse, as he finished his rounds, and I saw him loading another set of painkillers into the IV tree.

He gazed at me, and his eyes felt like they were shining into my soul. "I'd say a couple more days… you're stable now, but we're still watching you pretty closely."

I leaned back. I had nothing to do but wait, which was the opposite of what I wanted to do. I wanted to find where Jem was and help her out of what she was going through, but there was nothing I could do for the moment. I couldn't even call her, my phone was–

My phone. The nurse had said my phone had been on me when I'd been found. I could feel my eyelids getting heavy, but there was an urgency in my words that got the nurse's attention as he headed from the room. He turned to look at me again.

"My phone?" I asked.

"It's on the charger next to you on the bedside table."

I turned to look at it. Whoever had owned it, it wasn't mine. I'd had a large capacitive touchscreen, a late model thing that was in a shockproof case from all the times I'd dropped it on nightclub floors. The phone next to me was small and in a plastic case, with a physical dial pad and a two-fifty-six colour screen that had no touch capacity. It looked, as I suppose it was, like a drug dealer's burner phone.

I struggled to reach for it, and I got to it with my left hand, careful not to dislodge any of the medical equipment sticking from my arm. I pressed the unlock button, careful to not let it slip from my hands as I navigated through the antiquated menu screen.

I clicked the call log and there was only one - the outgoing dial to the emergency number that had presumably been placed to pick me up. I backed out of it and navigated to the messages.

Again, there was only one, from an unknown number that was kept on private. I opened it up, and I knew that my career as a Spice trader was done in that moment.

NO MORE.
WE'LL BE WATCHING.

* * *

I had no further issues with my recovery, and a bit less than a week later I was allowed out. They wheeled me through the hospital doors, then allowed me my own time to stand up. I could, with crutches, though it would be a long time before I could run again, if ever. They asked if I needed a taxi, and I said that I'd appreciate that very much. As my red-haired nurse, whose name I'd never bothered to learn, went inside to organize transport for me, I saw a lean, bearded figure get out of a car in the carpark.

He stared me down, and I could feel the threat in his eyes. I couldn't tear myself away from them. He was waiting for me to give me some sort of indication that I understood, and that I knew. I was under surveillance. Not by the police. Not by the state, and not by anyone who could claim to have my well-being at heart. I was being watched by a gang. A group of criminal thugs that made their livelihood by preying on the addictive side of the human psyche. They were watching me to make sure I never became their competition again. They needed me to understand that next time I wouldn't wake up in hospital. And they would know, because they had infiltrated those places that only mean the best for you, and they had chosen to revoke my right to privacy.

I stared at him, and I nodded slowly. *I understand,* the nod said. He nodded slowly back and held my stare.

"Taxi is on its way." The nurse was back again. I turned away from the stare to thank him, and by the time I turned back the man had climbed back into his car and was reversing from the parking lot.

"Do you need anything else?" The red-haired man asked.

"What? Uh, no. I'm fine. Thanks." I watched the nurse go, and then realised that there was one thing in the reception area he could grab for me. I got his attention and asked if I could have it before I left. He looked at me quizzically but complied.

When the taxi arrived, I clambered in awkwardly and threw my crutches into the back seat. I sat in the front next to the cabby, who recited my address to me. I told him a different one. He turned down a different street, and we didn't talk for the rest of the trip.

Chapter 22

I t had taken me longer than I would have liked to get up the uncovered flight of stairs in the concrete canyon between the two apartment blocks. I really hoped my visit wouldn't be in vain, and that something would have changed in the time since I'd last been here.

I knocked at the door, leaning carefully on my crutches and waiting. I heard a shuffling, and the sound of two or three latches being unlocked.

Jem's face appeared from behind the door, and her hazel eyes burst open in surprise when she saw me. She looked me up and down in shock, then said "Pete, what are you doing here?"

I gestured with one of my crutches . "Can I come in?"

She hesitated. "Pete, normally I would be fine with it, but the place is like, really messy. I've had a really rough couple of days and I–"

"Jem," I said sharply, then mellowed. "It's okay. I know."

She stared embarrassed at the ground. I watched the thoughts run through her head as she tried to make more excuses to not let me inside, but she couldn't, and she knew it. She relented and pulled the door back to let me in.

Manoeuvring through the doorway without crutches was difficult, but I managed to do it without too much hassle. Once

I was in, my heart sank.

All over the ground were used up wrappers and roaches from joints. There was a stench of marijuana in the air. The curtains were drawn, and all that was shedding light in the room was a single lamp on a side table next to the lounge. There were filthy clothes all over the floor, and the sofa had a grimy blanket and pillow that hadn't been washed laying on top of it. There were tiny baggies of all kinds of drugs and wraps from various others all over the coffee and side table. A glass pipe sat next to the sink. Worst of all were the needles. I saw several sitting on the counter. She'd been able to steal them from her work, and they now lay next to burnt spoons and exhausted tealight candles.

When I looked back at her, she seemed almost ready to cry.

"Can I sit down?" I said, and she gestured to the seats on the kitchen island. I sat in one, and she lowered herself carefully into the other. She looked at the scars on my face and opened her mouth to speak, but I stopped her.

"It's okay. I'll tell you," I said. "But then, you're going to tell me." I gestured broadly to the room, and she nodded.

Before I started, I took both of our phones. I wrapped them in towels and put them in the bathroom cupboard. Jem was eyeing me strangely when I got back, but then I told her everything that had happened since she'd disappeared on me that day. I told her about visiting the hospital to try and find her. I told her about how I thought the police were tracking me, so I'd run away to try and hide. How I'd realised my mistake and threw my phone out, but by then it was too late. I skipped over the worst of the details about the gang, but the violence was writ large all over my broken body. I didn't skimp away from the fact that I'd nearly been left for dead. It was only the threat that the attack might be traced back to the dealers that had left me alive.

I stared into her eyes as I finished the story; the hazel eyes that only a few weeks ago I'd sunk into and found joy losing myself in.

"Jem. We're done. We can't be in that world anymore. We need to make our way into normal society. No more Spice. No more drug dealing. No more anything. We have to come clean."

Her eyes were glistening with tears in the lamplight, and I noticed for the first time that what I'd mistaken for tiredness wasn't that. It was the beginnings of the hollow eyes of a heroin junkie. I'd finally made the connection when the dealers had denied knowing where she was. She hadn't been kidnapped... she'd gone to get a hit. And she'd been going away and getting hits for days at a time long before the Spice had been something that we could have been concerned about. All the times I tried to call her and she hadn't picked up she'd been lying on a grubby mattress somewhere, juiced up to her eyeballs. What's more, I was pretty sure I knew something else.

"You robbed Pat's house, didn't you?" I said, and I looked her in the eyes as I asked it. Her bottom lip trembled, and she broke down.

"Yes, I did. He was dead and I didn't know what to do, and the contacts I had weren't coming through with anything for me. When we'd gone and collected the stuff from his house, I'd seen the trays of drugs and I *knew* the police would just take it and destroy it if they went through his house." She was blubbering now, her face a rain of tears. "I knew that it would be too obvious if it was just the drugs that got taken, so I ransacked the entire place, but I had to leave in a hurry when I heard you pull up, so I didn't get to the lounge room."

So she'd been there *as I was entering the house*. "You made a mistake." I said.

She wiped her eyes, "What?"

"I said you made a mistake. You took the cider too. There was only beer in the fridge when I looked in there. You stole the drugs *and* the alcohol, but only the alcohol you liked. When I realised you had a habit, I made the connection because you stole the cider out of the fridge, but not the beer."

She laughed, a dismal, quiet sound that ran through the sobs momentarily before the crying caught up again, "Well, shit, Pete. Don't you know me so well."

Not well enough, I thought, "And whenever you disappeared for a few days, you'd be rubbing your arms together. I thought it was just a nervous tic, but now I know it was the track marks from the heroin." I shot daggers at her, then looked over at the burned spoons in the sink. "Wasn't it?"

She nodded again. I hadn't meant for it to happen, but I was getting angry. "You did this despite our deal. We were going to make sure that what happened to Pat *never happened to anyone we could help ever again!* You agreed to start making Spice with me to help others get over the substances that killed our best friend, meanwhile you were *fucking well taking them yourself!*" I tried to stand up but failed. My legs were killing me from the walk up the stairs, and the stitches on my face were hurting from shouting. I felt my cheek and looked at my fingers. I'd split the scab. It was bleeding again.

"I'm *sorry,*" Jem burst out at me. "I didn't know it had happened until it was far too late! I started on the harder stuff not long after Pat did, but I was telling myself I could keep it under control. I thought I could, and I think I was doing well!

But then Pat died and like…" Her face was streaming with tears, and her frail form was desperately leaning out to me. "I *loved* Pat. I *loved* him, and I love you. The two of you are my brothers. My family. My *home.* You're the only two people in my life who have always been there for me and then in the moment that it happened *I wasn't there for him.* I didn't know what the fuck to do, and the days after I needed to escape, and I knew it was there. I knew it was there and I took it." She hung her head, and her hair fell in front of her face.

"And you kept taking it." I said.

She nodded again. "I kept meaning to get clean. I really did. I would be fine but then I'd be out dealing spice or trying to drum up business or, fuck, just alone at night and thinking about Pat and I'd get offered a hit and I'd take it. I wasn't strong enough. I was never strong enough."

We sat in silence for some time after that. I don't really remember how long. I think we both zoned out a little, and we calmed ourselves down in our own quiet ways.

I spoke first, and I kept my tone conciliatory and level as I told her about my proposal. She reacted in surprise to some of the information I told her, but after I went through it all thoroughly, she took it on board. I offered to make the call for her, but she insisted she take the first step herself. I agreed, even if it turned out to only be symbolic, it meant a lot that she decided to deal with it on her own terms.

I handed her the magazine I'd asked the nurse to take from the waiting room at the hospital.

Chapter 23

We were outside, and the sun had finally peeked out from behind the spring clouds. I would always walk with a limp now; I knew after I'd finally ditched the crutches. The damage in my thigh muscle had been substantial, and a large chunk of it had to be taken out; it had gotten infected after the guys had ground their boots into it. Likewise, my cheeks would always look like I was in a horror movie, but I didn't mind so much about that.

The grass was bright green in the garden outside the two-storey facility, and there were a couple of small fountains. If I'd been a flower person, I would have no doubt appreciated the smells in the garden and the colours present everywhere. My mind couldn't help but wander as I felt the warm sun on my skin, and I was only brought out of my reverie when Kelly Gordon brought me back with a mention of my name.

"Peter?" she asked, and it was clearly the second or third time she'd done so.

"Oh, sorry? What was that?"

Kelly *tsk*ed at me, then said, "I was just asking if she was coming back to stay with you?"

"Oh. Yes. I think that'd be for the best. Her old place might make her relapse. Plus, I've moved. Might be a fresh start for her." I hadn't been able to stay in the house anymore. There were too many bad memories, and even though I knew I was being tracked, I felt safer in a place that had never had a note slipped under the door.

"Good," Kelly said, and it was clear that she thought it was for the best as well.

Kelly had had absolutely no questions when Jem had made the call some months ago on how to enroll in a rehabilitation program. She'd had the fierceness in her eyes brought back by the time it had come to go in, and I knew she'd give it everything to try and kick the habit.

I'd had an easier time. The direct threat of death if you ever knowingly go back into the drug trade ever again makes it easy to get over the need for a buzz. I'd called Kelly myself after a couple of weeks and asked if there was a counselor I could talk to that wasn't her. The counselor had turned out to be a very good decision and had helped when I needed to get through the worst of the withdrawals.

The doors to the facility opened, and I saw a shock of black hair pop out. Kelly waved her hello and Jem trotted down the steps and jumped into my arms. I never wanted that hug to end, and I kept myself pressed to her body. She'd put on weight, and the darkness was gone from around her eyes. I finally pulled back.

"Congratulations," I said. "You did it!"

"Thanks," she said, "They wanted to give me a sobriety chip, but I decided against it. I'm not going to count days. I'm just going to take them."

Kelly came over and congratulated her, and the two of them started talking about how the program had gone. I watched them interact, and I realised that I was no longer the only person in her life that wouldn't have given up on her now. Kelly was so invested into her well-being that she had genuinely befriended her in her time in rehab. I found myself smiling.

Jem had used all her Spice proceeds to buy drugs, so she wouldn't have been able to afford the rehab facility. I'd gone into the abandoned parking lot and found the letterbox where I'd stashed the cash. It had covered a fair proportion of it, but I was willing to pay the remainder out of my salary. We never discussed it with Jem.

I hadn't been able to get the money before the cash limit law got in place, but Kelly had backdated the payment for me. I couldn't help but wonder if she knew how I'd gotten the money, or whether she'd care if she did.

Jem bounded over, and grabbed me by the arm. "I hear you got a new house?" she grinned, and when I nodded at her, "Let's go see it!"

We turned to go, and I was acutely aware of Kelly watching us as we walked off together.

Jem stopped suddenly and turned around. "Oh shit, Pete. I forgot to say thank you! I'm just going to run and thank her; can you wait here?"

"Sure," I said.

"Oh, and Pete?"

"Yeah?"

"Thank *you* for doing this," she said. "I love you."

A moment froze between us. She was the closest thing I had to family now, and I could tell she meant it like that. It hadn't been resolved whether sleeping together had been a one off or a regular thing. These things could all be sorted in the future. But for now, I knew what I could say.

"I love you too, Jem."

She grinned and ran down the road. I watched after her, then turned away to allow the moment some privacy. I put my hand in the pocket of my jeans and felt a small rectangular piece of warm metal inside. I pulled it out. It was my zippo lighter.

Pat had given it to me as an urge to go out and do more, and do better, and do what you could to be a good person. I'd convinced myself that dealing Spice was doing that. I told myself that I was doing everything in my power to do the best I could, but that had been a lie.

In the end, sometimes you couldn't save the world. You could only truly save yourself. For all the calamity that happened everywhere, it was only in the quiet recesses of your mind that real, world-changing ideas could take place. So you had to take your own mind, and you had to make it into the best thing it could possibly be, and you had to do it in a way that made your impact on the world as positive as it could be.

Perfection is approachable.

I hadn't smoked in almost a month. The jeans had been through the wash, and as I flipped the lighter open I noticed it had become waterlogged. The incorrect Latin inscription on the side was now gone, and the utility of the thing had been washed away as much as its message had.

I walked over to a nearby tree and nestled it in the crook of the three major branches. I set it upright, to stand vigil, to hopefully help the others in the rehab center to save themselves as well.

I gazed around at the grounds, and my eyes caught sight of him. A bald man, bearded, with tattoos on his head, was watching me. Always watching me. My life was marked. A single movement out of line, and I would be hunted down and the job they started in the housing estate would be finished.

The scars on my face, the damage to my leg, and the death of my friend would weigh on me forever. There was a black mark on my body and soul, but it was the looming threat of retribution that would truly haunt me.

I hobbled back and waited on the path. Jem walked back toward me, watching me with quiet, sad eyes. We didn't need to say anything to each other. We knew.

We linked arms and she helped me limp back to the car.

About the Author

Henry Neilsen hails from Melbourne, Australia. After working as a sound technician, a factory worker, an oyster farmer and myriad other odd jobs, he went to university and studied architecture. He found out that he was rubbish at architecture and now works as a consultant in an engineering firm. When he isn't writing, he is a keen competitive rower who has competed at the Australian national championships. He writes speculative and science fiction, or at the very least stories with a speculative bent to them. He lives with his fiancee Anna and their two cats, Penelope and Ser Pounce.

You can connect with me on:
- http://www.huntingsunrise.com
- https://twitter.com/HuntingSunrise
- https://www.instagram.com/hunting_sunrise

Subscribe to my newsletter:
- http://www.huntingsunrise.com/mailing-list

Also by Henry Neilsen

Eleanor's Mind

Eleanor wakes up alone, in a near-featureless room with no windows or doors. A voice speaks to her from an unseen source: she's been in a car accident, and her mind has been transferred to a computer for safekeeping. Her body is being kept in an emergency room of a hospital while they heal her, and her brain function stopped some time ago.

The medical and computer teams are working around the clock to heal Eleanor's body, and to keep her mind from deteriorating inside the computer. Nobody has ever done this before; can they reunite the brain with the body again, or is Eleanor doomed to being locked in the computer generated room forever?